I0661360

W. Watman Smith

Echoes of the Past, Present, and Future

With other Poems

W. Watman Smith

Echoes of the Past, Present, and Future
With other Poems

ISBN/EAN: 9783337158514

Printed in Europe, USA, Canada, Australia, Japan

Cover: Foto ©Andreas Hilbeck / pixelio.de

More available books at **www.hansebooks.com**

ECHOES

OF THE

PAST, PRESENT, AND FUTURE.

With other Poems.

BY

W. WATMAN SMITH.

LONDON:

TRUBNER & CO., 8 & 60, PATERNOSTER ROW.

1870.

INDEX.

PREFACE.

As a head without a heart may be compared to a soul without a body, so a book without a preface may allegorically be said to resemble a ship without a pilot : what a pilot is to a ship, a preface is to a book ; and as the former often saves the ship from foundering, so the latter frequently preserves the book from slumbering in neglect on the shelf.

The Title Deeds of this property belong to many proprietors, who may figuratively be termed the freeholders of the ground upon which from time to time have been erected the several edifices which compose the titles of this work.

The division of the major poem into three parts, with their arrangement, was planned by the author, who alone is responsible for the metrical composition. In a short poem it would be utterly impossible to give more than a brief outline of the important themes it embraces, any one part of which possesses materials sufficient to swell a folio; nor would an elaborate treatise on one or all, be suitable for a poetical work, however interesting in a prose one.

Some critics will take exception to the adoption of the simple lyric measure, and think that blank verse would have been more appropriate for such a composition, inasmuch as it affords more freedom of thought than cramped rhymes admit of, and if not so musical, is at once more stately and eloquent. I must confess that 'half of that opinion's also mine,' but when the fragmentary sketches were first conceived, it was not contemplated that this bantling of the Muse would have grown to the stature it has since assumed, or the style would not have been adopted. As however we live in a prosaic and not in a poetical age, when a hundred readers of prose may be counted for one of poetry, it may possibly entice some by its attractive form and titles to open the infant volume, while blank verse would probably have condemned it as a sealed book.

Poetry has been eclipsed by Prose since the days of Byron, Scott, Rogers, Moore, Campbell, Shelley, Wordsworth, Coleridge, and gone out of fashion like the drama, which has given place to the opera : if the reason is sought, the simple answer is that either taste has changed, or that we have few good living poets. I am inclined to believe in the last supposition rather than the first, for, with the advance of education, the number of readers of light literature such as novels has steadily increased, as well as of works of more solid and useful instruction.

If asked what are the elements that constitute poetry ? the question may be laconically answered by saying not rhymes alone, which are mere versifications to give a musical sound to the ear ; these, however sweet and harmonious, unless they embody feeling and fancy, with a special intellectual faculty of mind, cannot contain the true essence of poetry. To be original and creative requires genius, which may be cultivated and improved.

Poetry is nearly as old as prose, and is found scattered over all nations, barbarous or civilized ;

it is the diction of the improvisatore and minstrel; and has also been described as the language of passion and vivid imagination, as in songs and hymns of praise, liberty, triumph or sorrow.

Cold climates seem to freeze up the imagination, while the warm sunbeams kindle and inspire it. The beauties of nature charm the sight as glowing sunshine cheers it, and thence draw upon the fancy for comparisons, along with the imitative arts. Love is a powerful incentive to arouse the passions, while rural and mountain scenery present us with pleasing landscapes and poetical pictures.

Music and melody, with figurative language, emblems, and metaphors, are the graces of composition, and adorn the writings of our best poets. Blank verse, the epic, and tragedy, are considered the most stately and dignified, and come nearer to the prosaic style of composition than all others. The Hebrew poetry of scripture is full of imagery, sublime sentiments, and exalted ideas, which constitute true poetry; such also are the works 'Ossian,' the 'Messiah', and 'Telemachus'.

A great book has long been pronounced a great evil, and therefore if this dwarf possesses no other recommendation, it will have the merit of being brief, and containing *multum in parvo*, or thoughts for study. We hear of times gone by when authors composed their twenty thousand lines in a poem ; but we do not seek to build up such a pyramid and to weary the reader with a superfluous quantity of letter-press in times like the present, so fruitful of book publications awaiting the leisure of the reader, but to condense in a small compass the work in question : besides trying his patience, his daily avocations would prevent him giving the necessary time for perusing works of magnitude, so peculiar to our forefathers who had more leisure to write, read and digest, than we of the present toiling generation.

In the Alpha and Omega of the principal poem, we have been obliged to draw largely upon the imagination ; for the revelations of prophets, poets and divines throw a very glimmering light upon the past of History, or the future of our destiny. Man hopes and instinctively believes in a spiritual existence hereafter, and in a forgiving and merciful, rather than in a cruel and revengeful Deity.

The Miscellaneous effusions are mostly living pictures of the scenes and incidents they describe, and their composition scattered over a period of many years, drawn while fresh in the memory, and are chiefly moral, pathetic, and descriptive.

THREE Sages pass before me in my dream
   Different in genius, character, and face,
   United with the links of Time and Space,
In high priest's robes.   Like oracles they seem,
The Past revealing and the Future scheme
   Of Providence, foreshadowing to sight,
   Creation's wonders with the infinite
And Past of Ages, lost in Lethe's stream!
   They too unroll Time's hieroglyphic screen;
    And all obliterated things restore,
   With the great drama of life's shifting scene
    Now Present, and th' invisible far shore,
     In the horizon of Eternity,
     Which dimly shadows the Soul's destiny.

THE PAST,

OR

CREATION, NATURE AND DEITY.

ANALYSIS.

PART I.

Invocation to the Muse—Creation—The planetary Systems
of the Universe—Nature's God—Earth—Infinity—
Eternity of the Past—The Pre-adamite Earth—The
Great Deluge— Nature — The Seasons — Heavenly
Bodies—Divine contemplation—Speculative Inquiry—
Review of Ancient Nations—Ruins—Deity.

OH ! Lyric Muse ! thy glory shed
    Around me and inspire !
Celestial influence o'er me spread,
    And tune my sacred lyre !

While I attempt a loftier theme,
    And search out Nature's plan ;
Which unrevealed appears a dream
    And mystery to Man !

B

Of the ethereal and sublime,
　　Divinely let me sing !
Of things anterior to Time,
　　Or man's imagining.

From local scenes let us ascend
　　The Universe to trace !
From finite being comprehend
　　The infinite of Space !

Oh ! for a telescopic mind
　　Creation to look through !
And undiscovered Worlds to find
　　All open to our view !

Rise from this groveling world below
　　Of anxious care ;—ascend
To Nature's gallery and show !
　　And systems without end !

The Universe expanded lies,—
　　Immensity's wide range :
There 's life and motion in the skies,
　　With panoramic change.

Whence did this Exhibition spring !
   Vast, wondrous and sublime !
Can sages say or poets sing
   Its birth, foundation, time ?

We meditate amongst the stars,—
   Their origin would know,
From distant Uranus to Mars,
   Around, above, below.

Like clock machinery all seem
   On chains and wheels to turn :
Perpetual motion is no dream,
   Its action we discern.

Thousands of Solar systems rise
   In the broad arch of night ;
And myriads more are hid in skies
   Beyond the reach of sight !

Yon sister spheres that picture night
   In luminous array ;
Whence drew they being ?—first saw light !
   Across the ethery way ?

All active and revolving there,
   Suspended in the Heaven,
Some purpose serve, and all declare
   A vital influence given.

As all the systems of the sky,
   Have each their central sun ;
Creation has its Deity,
   With whom all worlds begun.

God formed Creation ! whence sprang He ?
   When, where, and how produced ?
Profound, eternal mystery !
   Which all things introduced !

A Being infinite as Space,
   Which fancy can't conceive !
But whose omniscience we can trace
   Through Nature and believe !

Were we to soar to any star,
   That lights the spacious skies ;
We might by search discover far,
   The Earth ! a ball in size,

Minutely small amidst the host
   Of planets in the air ;
Circling its Sun, and almost lost
   Mid constellations there.

The broad back'd Ocean looks a blot
   The highest mountain low :
The widest continent a dot :
   The whole a speck below.

A dwarfish crawling biped* there.
   For optics too minute,
Is busied with a world of care,
   Instinctive to the brute.

The zodiacal signs we trace
   Of heaven's celestial map,
And soar aloft through twilight Space.
   But find an endless gap.

The dizzy heights we now explore,
   In this aerial flight,
To scan Creation's roof and floor,
   Bewilder sense and sight.

* Man.

Infinity and endless sky,
  Dim the farsighted mind ;
Where ethery fields all open lie,—
  A vacuum unconfined.

Whence come and go with threat'ning glare,
  (Spreading alarm around,)
The wandering Comets of the air,
  Lost in the gulf profound ?

Mysterious auguries of Fate !
  The heralds of the sky !
Collision would annihilate
  A world in passing by.

A shower of meteors cross the sky,
  And shooting stars down fall,
By Earth attracted as they fly,
  Are atmospheric all.

The tinted rainbow smiles above,
  And lulls the storm to rest ;
As the soft melting eye of love,
  Tames down the savage breast.

What are those changeful skies but air,
   Through which our planet 's hurled ?
In rotatory motion there,
   On its own axis whirled ?

Eternity! cycles of years,
   Nor measurement define !
A hollow, dark abyss appears
   Where Systems cease to shine !

Ages of Time have rolled away
   Since first discerned by man !—
Eternal Ages since the day
   Creation's works began !

Our Earth was wrapt in blackest gloom !
   Still as the sleep of death !
Dense, cold and torpid as the tomb,
   Without life's vital breath !

Darkness sealed up the face of day,
   And clouds obscured the night ;
Lost in the firmament it lay
   Without a ray of light !

Before its elements were form'd,
    Th' embryo Earth was changed ;
For storms and hurricanes deform'd,—
    Convulsions disarranged.

Dark clouds hung on the brow of Heaven,
    A nightmare of the Earth,
Encompassed round, half wreck'd and driven,
    While struggling into birth.

At last a lamp appeared to rise,
    And dissipate the gloom ;
Unveiling all the glittering skies,
    Immured as in a tomb !

Darkness retreated ! clouds dissolved !—
    The vapoury curtains rose
As by enchantment ! and evolved,
    The radiant sphere disclose !

The mist of night recedes from shore,
    And the sun's light reveals
A hidden world unknown before !
    Which slept in ethery fields.

Cold, barren, dead, inanimate,
   For ages there it lay ;
An undigested mass of slate,
   Rock, water, limestone, clay !

Ere tree, shrub, flower, or greensward grew,
   Organic life began !
Or Nature's face dawn'd into view,
   Anterior to man !

Awakening from oblivious sleep,
   Our planet teems with life !
The earth, the air, the heavens, the deep,
   With living things are rife !

The birds pour forth their music sweet,
   The earth is robed with flowers ;
Warm'd with the sun's inspiring heat,
   And cloud-distilling showers.

Creation thus began to dawn,
   God's purpose to fulfil ;
And worlds with suns to light them born,
   Submissive to his will !

When the first Deluge drown'd the Earth,
    Which monsters wild o'erran ;
Man had not issued into birth,
    Nor order's laws began.

Earthquakes have rent the solid earth,
    Piecemeal, and fauna slain !
Their spectral ruins yawning forth,
    And fossil forms remain !

The agitated mountains burst,
    With labour pains of birth,
Struggling to penetrate the crust
    Of our volcanic Earth.

The partial Flood submerged the land,
    And left the deep sea dry !
The inland rocks memorials stand,
    And hills that pierce the sky.

The subterranean depths unfold
    The forest and the sea !
The extinct animals of old,
    Prove Earth's antiquity !

Antediluvian wrecks appear,
   And mines of fossil coal,
Marine remains found everywhere,
   And plants from pole to pole.

These transformed relics of blank date,
   Embodied in the Earth,
While in an embryonic state,
   Disclose their ancient birth.

They were the eldest born of Time,
   Growth of a distant Age ;
Long ere this planet reached its prime,
   Or Adam trod the stage.

A hundred thousand years or more,
   May bridge the gulf between
The earliest age of man, before
   The recent pliocene.

The flooding rains in torrents pour,
   The vivid lightnings flash !
The claps of thunder bursting roar,
   With an explosive crash !

The Ocean grapples with the wind,
　　Its waves in mountains roll ;
Its fury continents can't bind,
　　For it o'erwhelms the whole !

The foaming billows lash the shore,
　　The stormy tempests sigh,--
The upheaved mountains tumbling o'er,
　　Confused and scattered lie.

Night, anarchy, disorder, spread
　　And fill'd with groans the air ;
The elemental strife made head,
　　And Death stalked everywhere !

The Earth convulsed in pieces flew,
　　And rock'd and rolled with ire :
And its volcano mouths upthrew,
　　Columns of smoke and fire !

Explosions crack'd and whirlwinds roll'd
　　As if 'twere rent in twain !
It's drift and debris we behold,
　　In ruins that remain !

Fragments of rocks, bones, shells and trees,
   Were seething in the mud ;
Wash'd from all countries and all seas,
   Tossed by the angry flood !

Leviathans of monstrous form
   Lay struggling in the mire ;
And all,—all perished in the storm ;
   That rained stones, rocks, and fire !

What graveyards underlie the whole
   Earth's surface, pile on pile !
Slate, granite, sandstone, limestone, coal,
   Mammalia, fish, reptile !

Nature at last proclaims a truce,
   Exhausted, wild, distrest !
The raging elements let loose,
   Sink calmly into rest !

The Alps and Andes first arose,
   From their chaotic birth :
And subsequent convulsive throes,
   Have water logged the earth.

The waters settle or recede,
   The drown'd land reappears,
And useful animals succeed
   Th' extinct of former years.

A paradise of flowers and fruit,
   Perfume the balmy air ;
And ornamental trees take root,
   And flourish everywhere.

The risen Earth in rainbow skies,
   Looks green, fresh, young and fair :
And noble Man in Princely guise,
   Is God's vicegerent there !

The Seasons change as onward rolls
   Our planet round the Sun ;
And each its character unfolds,
   As through the Year they run.

The youthful Spring with garlands fair,
   Unveils her blushing face ;
Diffusing through the earth and air,
   Her gladd'ning smiles of grace.

Let heart rejoice ! returning Spring,
  Reanimates the Earth !
And all that has been slumbering,
  Revives,—renews its birth !

Who has not felt the joyous Spring
  With rapture throb his heart ?
Who has not heard his spirit sing,
  And joining take a part ?

Sweet Summer's warm inspiring rays,
  Bring on her charming flowers ;
And minstrel birds pour out their lays,
  From Eden's happy bowers.

The fruitful Autumn ! ripe, serene,
  Draws on her twilight shade ;
And tints the foliage changing green,
  As youth and beauty fade.

Stern Winter ! desolate and cold !
  Is capp'd in ice and snow ;
Inanimate, dark, nude, and old,
  Wears Time upon his brow !

How Life is typified by all !
　　How like its Seasons change !
Its morning rise,—its evening fall !
　　And evanescent range !

Creation's wondrous works we view
　　With deep emotion here :
And feel exalted searching through
　　The Heavens and our own sphere.

The kindred orbs that o'er us roll,
　　Mysterious and sublime !
Abstract the contemplative soul,
　　From transient things of Time !

Who can that starry dome survey,
　　And musing not admire ?
Who would not if he could convey
　　Himself to regions higher ?

The flight of fancy cannot soar
　　Beyond the orb-fill'd sky ;
Or follow the receding shore
　　Of dark Eternity !

Regions of solitude lie there,
  Blank, desert-like to view ;
Perpetual night and breathless air :
  With firmament of blue.

Our plebeian thoughts confined to Earth,
  Contracted to a span,
Determine not their dateless birth,
  Or the Creator's plan !

The mind that 's circumscribed by Time,
  And history of our race :
Conceives nought of those works sublime
  Which populate all space !

There 's wise arrangement and design
  Throughout the spacious whole ;
For globes opaque and suns that shine,
  Are subject to control !

The earliest times of man record
  Some knowledge of the sky :
Wizards with cabalistic word
  Reveal'd futurity.

The hieroglyphic symbols there,
    Astrologers translate !
Prophetic Sybils there repair,
    To learn our earthly Fate !

These preternatural divines,
    Agents 'twixt heaven and earth,
Magicians seem, whose occult signs
    Gave Superstition birth.

Egypt ! Greece ! Rome ! viewed and admired
    The firmament above !
And glowing poets felt inspired,
    Rapt in Platonic love.

Roam through the broad expanse of Night !
    The star-sown sky survey !
What showers of gold-dust crowd the sight,
    Far as the Milky Way !

Through the tube's magnifying glass,
    Behold the galaxy !
How some in brilliancy surpass !
    What strata 'bove them lie !

There's Saturn with his numerous zones
    Of wind and amber light !
And Jupiter with all his moons,
    Like sentinels of Night.

The clust'ring Pleiades afar,
    As if in concert met !
And sailors' friendly pilot star,
    Deep in the north-sky set !

How radiant beams the Eye of Day,
    On all the globes around !
How life and nature would decay
    To-morrow if not found !

Serenely calm the Queen of Night
    Sails through the concave skies !
An area grand and infinite,
    Beaming with lustrous eyes !

Awakening Day,—reposing Night,
    Wheel round from Age to Age
Alternately, and shew Time's flight
    Upon the dial's page !

How small the space these distant orbs
   Fill in the vaulted sky!
Th' unfathomed void abstracts, absorbs
   The contemplative eye!

Their origin? and how produced?
   Their author?—use?—and end?
Did Chaos always reign confused?
   And world on world depend?

Does that dim vapoury mist on high,
   Refuge of matter,—scum,—
Grow dense and hard within the sky,—
   A living World become?

Is it an offshoot of the Sun?
   Or atoms that adhere?
Of varied elements, and spun
   By motion into sphere?

Had matter any pristine shape?
   Was space the void we see?
From whence did wind, storm, air, escape?
   And dim Eternity?

Was there Beginning?—is there End?
  Can finite creature say?
Or the world's wisdom comprehend.
  And solve the problem, eh?

Can depth of thought, or sages fix
  The periods of their birth?
Do the same elements commix
  There, as compose our Earth?

Are worlds inhabited above?
  By man, or angel race,
United in the bonds of love,
  Or empty globes of Space?

If peopled, are they half divine,
  With body and a soul?
Do they their mortal part resign?
  The spiritual them control?

Does vice their nature e'er pollute?
  Has sin found entrance there?
Is man the tyrant, slave, and brute,
  He has been found elsewhere?

Or are they formed of purer clay ?
    With gentler passions born ?
Doth the night interchange with day ?
    And the four Seasons warn ?

Are they of rough or finer mould,
    As distant from the Sun ?
T' endure th' extremes of heat and cold,
    Our feeble natures shun ?

In scorched-up climes to suns so near,
    That water is not found ?
Or so remote, the rolling year
    In ice and snow is bound ?

Can finite knowledge comprehend
    The infinite and vast ?—
Our cultured faculties ascend
    The heights where worlds are cast ?

Do they our Earth take into view,
    And cross the bridge of Time ?—
These philosophic thoughts pursue,
    Inspired with the sublime ?

Have they the same inquiring mind
   And faculties as we ?—
As curious to explore and find
   Out more than they can see ?

How pass they and beguile their Time ?
   Is life a round of years ?
Have birds, beasts, insects, fish, a clime
   In yonder rolling spheres ?

Do sunny landscapes feast the sight,
   And groves and gardens smile,
The soul bewitching with delight,
   As through this past'ral isle ?

Some narrow minds in little men,
   This vein of thought would bind ;
And shut these visions from our ken,
   Or manacle the mind.

Exalted Reason will inquire,
   (God's noblest gift to man !)
And elevate a little higher
   His chef-d'œuvre if it can !

Nature has stereotyped on all,
    That all who breathe must die ;
And all that rises up must fall ;
    It is their destiny !

Who has not felt within him glow
    Th' impulsive Soul's desires ?
And his best feelings overflow,
    When music's voice inspires ?

Nature ! thy sweet pictorial charms,
    With rapture fill my breast !
Oh ! I could rush into thy arms,
    And there contented rest !

The deep-toned Ocean's anthem swells,—
    The voice of Nature sounds ;
A vital essence inward dwells,
    In all that us surrounds.

The Mountain of stern solitude
    Sits regally on high ;
And beacons, torn by tempests rude,
    Watch Ages passing by !

The grandeur of the lightning's glare,
   Th' artillery of Heaven ;
The earthquake's throes which rend and tear,
   And stormy tempests driven,

Attest the presidence of God !
   And genius Divine !
Sinai was once his brief abode,
   And Nature's face his shrine !

How Time withdraws and veils from view
   The Nations of the Earth !
If we its chronicles look through,
   Few long survive their birth !

Their memories flash across the mind,
   Like shadows of a dream
That haunt us when we wake and find
   Them bubbles on life's stream.

Babylon ! Nineveh ! Judea !
   Lie prostrate in the grave ;
With all their Kings and Priests held dear,
   The proud !—the great !—the brave !

Entomb'd near mount Vesuvius' feet,
  In ashes Pompeii
And Herculaneum almost meet,
  Forgot, unknown, pass'd by !

O'er proud Jerusalem we mourn !
  On its famed Temple gaze !
And cities no less glorious born,
  And great in ancient days.

Palmyra ! in the desert lies,
  A relic of the past !
And ruins of the great arise,
  All blotted out at last !

Phœnicia ! Petra ! India ! Tyre !
  Recall the days of yore !
With Persia in her silk attire,
  And Arab's spicy shore !

Syria and holy Palestine !
  Th' celestial of the earth !
Oppress'd with Moslem's yoke decline,
  But have a phœnix birth.

Egypt's proud Pyramids survive
 T' immortalize her name !
And sacred in our memory live,
 Her temples and her fame !

Illustrious Greece ! to bards divine,
 And orators gave birth ;
Her monuments the great enshrine !
 And wisdom of the Earth !

Imperial and all conquering Rome !
 The world knelt at thy feet ;
Till luxury debauch'd thy home,
 And vice usurp'd thy seat.

Imagine an anterior Age,
 With nations gone before !
Reveal their history,—con the page,
 And countries lost deplore !

The sleeping cities of the dead,
 An empire's dust contain :
Youth, beauty, wealth and rank have fled,
 Their memories but remain !

Cyrus and Xerxes pass in view
 Down Time's oblivious tide !
Cæsar and Alexander too,
 Whose conquering arms spread wide !

Power and distinction underlie
 The tombstones of the ground :
No dust of their mortality,
 Is in Death's chambers found.

Old relics of a former age,
 The learned still admire,
While poring o'er the antique page,
 Or 'mongst their sights inquire.

Sacred to thought ! to memory dear,
 Are remnants of the past !
In sympathy we drop a tear,
 When life is ebbing fast !

Is everything to ruin doom'd,
 An universal wreck ?
Will all decay or be consum'd ?
 And Time not leave a speck ?

Shall worlds decline and pass away,
   And leave no trace behind
Of kingdoms great !—and mortal clay !
   By monuments enshrin'd ?

Shall this Earth e'er extinguish'd be ?
   Its elements dissolve ?
And chaos' rude antiquity
   In atoms all involve ?

Shall shores of time and oceans vast,
   Be driven from their place ?
Shall generated globes at last,
   Be swallowed up in Space ?

And who the last of mortal race,
   To see this change begun ?
When wrecks of worlds are hurled through space,
   And eclipsed is our Sun !

The laws of Nature govern all
   The Systems of the sky :
And in their orbits great and small,
   Rotate in harmony.

Each journeys round its central sun,
　　And on its axis rolls ;
Each has its daily course to run,
　　Where gravitation holds !

There is elaborate ~~and~~ design,
　　An architectural plan !
And He who form'd it a divine
　　Enigma is to man !

God's glorious works our eyes admire,
　　Till contemplation 's blind ;
We feel entranced while they inspire,
　　And captivate the mind !

The ignorance that us surrounds,
　　Is proof we little know
Beyond the verge of this world's bounds,
　　Fix'd as we are below.

Suppose man driven from this sphere !
　　The works he left behind,
Would indicate he had been here,
　　With his exalted mind !

And so Creation's works attest,
  Creator! though conceal'd;
Whose Spirit in the human breast,
  And Nature's face reveal'd.

Effects to causes let us trace,
  In proof of nature's laws,
And moral government embrace,
  Which springs from a first cause.

From Nature up to Nature's God,
  We naturally rise:
The Universe is his abode,
  Throughout the spacious skies!

Who could this wondrous scheme devise,
  Create, fix, form, control?—
Who launch those worlds into the skies,
  But Him who heads the whole?

In solemn Majesty sublime,
  From his exalted throne,
Th' Eternal views the wrecks of Time,
  Throughout our planet shewn.

His goodness, power and wisdom fill
   The Universe around.
Through Science all may trace his skill,
   Who rules the vast profound!

Creation infinite obeys
   Omnipotence divine;
And he must worship who surveys
   Heaven's Temple nightly shine!

The wide pictorial fields above,
   Absorb the studious mind;
And fill with homage, praise and love,
   The hearts of all mankind.

To bring down knowledge from the skies!
   Th' invisible to view!
Man's daring genius nobly tries
   To find out something new!

Creation's lord must still aspire,
   And wing his thoughts above;—
His intellectual mind inquire,
   After the God of love!

Heaven! Earth! immortal Man we trace,
　　To an Almighty hand!
But He who animated Space,
　　We fail to understand.

Before those stars created were,
　　Or local found their place;
God's spirit floated in the air,
　　His presence filled all space!

Essence miraculous! divine!
　　Nature's imperial soul!
In which all elements combine
　　In parts to form the whole!

God is a Spirit we are told!
　　Father of spirits too!
But where's the artist to unfold,
　　His image to our view?

He in his works is recognized,
　　Omniscient and sublime!
In them reveal'd and idolized,
　　Throughout all worlds and time!

D

Incomprehensible and great !
    Invisible to all !
To live in all he does create,
    Is preternatural !

Were all the intellects of men,
    Of scattered worlds combined ;
They would not bear comparison,
    With God's all-knowing mind !

The unexpounded miracle
    Of wonder ! the first cause
Of all existence ! spiritual !
    Centre of souls and laws !

Mysterious ruling Providence !
    Who governs by his will ;
Inscrutable his ways to sense,
    An unsolved problem still !

We feel his influence here below !
    Discern it in the sky !
While not the meanest thing we know.
    Escapes his watchful eye !

His wisdom is beyond all praise,
   Of beings here below :
Yet man his humble voice will raise.
   His gratitude to shew !

Praise God from whom all blessings flow,
   And Nature's laws obey !
Fulfil your duties here below,
   And with devotion pray !

All reverence, worship, and adore,
   The undefined of all,
That's Spiritual ! and upward soar
   To one Original !

Father of all ! Eternal ! One !
   Impartial, just, and wise !
The source, the essence, mind and sun,
   Of all within the skies !

Let all the Earth in concert rise,
   And homage pay to Thee !
Great Ruler of the Earth and Skies !
   Unravell'd Mystery !

"Thy kingdom come" is still our prayer,
   Our longing, fond desire !
The future home we hope to share.
   To which our souls aspire !

From Thee we all first took our rise,
   Thy providence we share ;
We seek Thee in the inner skies,
   But find Thee everywhere !

Unseen, unknown, and yet confest,
   In every age and clime ;
Thy spirit dwells in every breast,
   Oracular ! Sublime !

The Universe is full of thee !
   Most wonderful, profound ;
Ubiquitous o'er space, we see
   Thy presence all around !

Author of being ! source of light !
   Of Nature and of Man !
The Universe displays thy might !
   Creation is thy plan !

THE PRESENT,

OR

MAN, THE WORLD, AND THEOLOGY.

PART II.

Man, his primitive and civilized state—Time Present—
England—Modern discoveries—The Old World—Pro-
gression — Intellect — Art — Science — Death — Theo-
logies—Bible—Jesus and other luminaries—The great
Eternal—Creeds—Priestcraft—Religion.

ANGEL of light, thy grace impart
　　To my deep thirsting mind !
Teach, guide, and stimulate my heart
　　Thy sacred porch to find !

Oh ! fill my soul with beams divine,
　　Thy seraph form to see !
Unveil thy face and on me shine,
　　Handmaid of Deity !

With lark-like warblers of the sky,
   Who carol on the wing,
My soul in ecstacy would fly,—
   In cloudless heav'ns to sing!

God's greatest—noblest work is Man!
   Creation's youngest birth!
The last link in the general plan!
   God's image upon earth!

Of all conceived ideas the best,
   With attributes divine:
Beyond all living creatures blest,
   Where light and wisdom shine!

Man seems an instrument of power,—
   An agent to fulfil
The schemes of Providence! a tower
   Of strength to do His will.

The Lord reveals himself to man,
   In whispers to all hearts;
Through conscience since the race began,
   He communes and imparts!

His mental faculties and brain,
  Genius and power attest!
The windings of the nerve and vein,
  And wave-tides of the breast!

The symmetry,—reflective face,—
  The lungs,—eye,—heart and hand,–
With senses which protect and grace
  The noblest creature plann'd!

Endowed with reason, sense and speech,
  Is proof of God's design
T" ennoble, elevate and teach,
  And rank him half divine.

In form, in spirit and address,
  Superior to all!
Placed here for what? the problem guess:
  To rise! fulfil! and fall!

Did he from rebel Angels spring,
  Half human, half divine?
Or is he such as poets sing,
  From father Adam's line?

Or from the elder simian race,
    Anatomists describe ?
The Physiologists him trace
    To the gorilla tribe.

Races of men pre-adamite
    Were scattered through the earth :
Their flint remains are brought to light,
    With brutes of monstrous birth.

Was he originally wild,
    As savage tribes are found ?
Or Nature's pet and darling child,
    Who smiled on all around ?

Vice, immorality and sin,
    Lead all mankind astray,
When untamed nature reigns within,
    And conscience scares away.

Affliction, madness, dire distress,
    All classes fill with gloom ;
While grief, and want, and wretchedness
    Pursue us to the tomb.

Labour, anxiety and care,
  Are stamp'd on every face,
Death, disappointment and despair,
  Crush, wound and scourge the race.

Misfortune, penury and age,
  Cast down the weary soul,
Now reconciled to quit the stage,
  For its translated goal.

How many would dissolve the tie,
  That binds the soul to earth ?
And like a chrysalis would lie,
  Till launched into new birth ?

If Angels sympathize above,
  With human suffering here,
'Tis proof that mercy, grace and love,
  Flow from their councils there.

Lo ! primitively wild and rude,
  He wanders on the shore,
Fishing the streams and hunting food,
  Like nomad tribes before.

We find him on the barren coast,
   Unfathom'd seas divide ;—
On isles remote, in oceans lost,—
   He migrates far and wide.

We trace him through Earth's varied climes,
   In language, colour, race ;
From modern up to early times,
   In wild and cultured place.

In barb'rous slavery confin'd,
   And brutal ignorance bred ;
Clouded with darkness is his mind,
   When by his passions led.

Ambition, war, lust, murder, stain
   And petrify his heart :
Heroes for glory,—kings for gain,
   Take their dramatic part !

Survey the busy hives of men,
   How each performs his part :
Their various employments ken,
   In nature and in art ; .

Shall savage war extinguish'd be,
    And cursed serfdom cease ?—
The wild be tamed ? the whole world free ?
    United and at peace ?

The world in miniature is shewn,
    Assembled at one view,
In the circumference of a town,
    Stirring with life all through.

Nature predominates o'er all,
    But custom schools us here ;
As constituted, great, and small,
    Fill their peculiar sphere.

Art, Science, Commerce pass in view,
    And vanities of life :
With hostile armies marching through,
    'Midst politician's strife.

Life's active duties still supply,
    A place for all to fill :
Trade, manufactures, tillage lie,
    All open to our skill.

Wealth, pleasure, fame, will not content,
 Nor pow'r or beauty bless ;
When youth and health and strength are spent,
 In servile worldiness.

There is a paradise above,
 A God to pray to here,
For mercy, peace of mind and love ;
 And our salvation there.

This world's a temporary sojourn,
 For wisest purpose giv'n ;
To train, refine, exalt and learn,
 Preparat'ry for heaven !

There seems, on superficial view,
 Injustice done to man :
Reflect and search th' enigma thro' ;
 Then censure if you can.

Birth, fortune, destiny and fate,
 Are riddles to the mind ;
And emblem forth life's chequered state,
 Capricious as the wind.

There must be different degrees,
　With rulers to command :
Law, constitution, order please,
　And socialize a land !

Life, property and sacred ties,
　And all he holds most dear,
Protection claim ! and hence man flies,
　To government 'tis clear !

Thus illustrated life appears,
　A stage to play a part,
In characters a few brief years ;
　Then one by one depart !

If we attempt to look Time through,
　Chronology is brief ;
And leaves of history so few,
　Doubt mingles with belief.

Time is made up of Ages past,
　Which present hours supply !
Its wrecks are graves and empires vast !
　We quit it when we die.

The undeveloped world will grow,
    Like youth from age to age ;
And infant states expanded so,
    In turn will tread the stage.

France, Russia, Germany, and Spain,
    May change but still be great ;
Or vestiges of Time remain,
    In a chaotic state.

Oh ! where will dear old England be ?
    And what her station then ?
The honoured birthplace of the free,—
    Th' asylum of all men !

Her restless children spread and root
    On many a foreign shore ;
And like a vigorous off-shoot,
    Their shadows cast before.

India, China, and Japan,
    Each with a swarming race !
Like infant colonies began,
    Ere they rank'd high in place.

All change with age, and some expire.
   Their ruined walls we find !
We like our ancestors retire,
   And leave our seed behind.

Another flood may sweep away !
   A volcano entomb !
Earthquake destroy ! or conqueror slay !
   O'er all there hangs a doom.

What is proud England's destiny ?
   Will she be ever great ?
Or Tyre-like of antiquity
   Succumb at last to fate ?

Age may add wrinkles to her brow !
   Her prestige disappear !
But memory of her glories now,
   Must make our country dear !

Her laurels Time will not efface,
   Her power it may subdue !
Her history shall survive, and race.
   Tho' sunk and lost to view.

Unknown, forgot, an Empire's dust,
   May lie entomb'd below,
Like Pompeii! another crust
   Our Island overgrow!

Some distant Age in her decline,
   Send pilgrims to our shore;
Some Marius o'er her sacred shrine,
   Weep, meditate, deplore!

New worlds are opening on our sight,
   Whose being was unknown,
Till Science shed her beams of light,
   And on a genius shone!

Three centuries scarce have closed their eyes.
   And open'd up to view
A Continent!—a world in size!
   With savage tribes all through.

A dark and spell-bound Hemisphere.
   Was first unveiled to light!
The two Americas lay there,
   Reveal'd to Europe's sight!

The trackless forest,—boundless plain,
    The mountain, prairie, stream ;
For unknown ages there had lain,
    A phantom ! myth ! and dream !

Disclosed to view Australia lies,
    A wilderness of wood :
And New South Wales, another prize,
    Rescued from solitude !

New Zealand ! Mexico ! Peru !
    Columbia and the sea,
Resemble a Creation new ;
    Nations in infancy !

The New World promises to be
    The rival of the Old !
Great, pow'rful, enterprizing, free.
    And rich in mines of gold.

The dreary regions of the Pole,
    Imperfectly we know :
In ice imprisoned is the whole,
    And everlasting snow !

'Tis thus from nature unrefin'd,
   Progressive man we trace ;
Who now unfolds the god-like mind
   Of his immortal race.

Rank, honor, title, wealth and fame,
   Mark th' illustrious great :
Castles and palaces and name,
   Give dignity and state.

Rich marble mosques and monuments,
   Mid towers and temples stand,
With pyramids to mark events,
   O'er all the eastern land.

The intellectual gifts of mind,
   The tongue of eloquence,
With imagery and taste combin'd,
   And cultured elegance,

Incline us to the sister arts,
   That elevate the soul ;
And stamp their image on our hearts,
   And soften and control.

Painting and Sculpture and design,
  Our admiration raise :
Music and poetry refine
  And fill with songs of praise.

The rich auriferous vein of thought,
  Embedded in the mind ;
By genius curiously is wrought,
  Adorn'd, enriched, refin'd !

From knowledge, truth and wisdom spring,
  Genius and learning shine :
To contemplate 's a noble thing,
  Inspiring and divine !

What from the ancients was conceal'd,
  Of star-lit heaven and earth,
To us lies open and reveal'd,
  And have a modern birth.

Columbus mapp'd the unknown Sea,
  And Newton measured Space ;
Impell'd,—inspired by Deity,
  Who guides our sovereign race !

Discoveries have open'd wide
   The knowledge of mankind ;
And must with Reason be the guide
   And compass of our mind.

Each Age adds wisdom and new light
   Unto the fruitful past :
The telescope expands our sight !
   The printing type is cast !

Astronomy has much reveal'd,
   And open'd up to sight
The springs of Nature long conceal'd,
   In barren fields of night.

Th' electric wires that cross the sea !
   The rail that girds the earth !
Gas, powder, guns, machinery,
   And steam of magic birth.

Geology has brought to light,
   The secrets of the past !
And giv'n with Chymistry insight
   To Nature's earth-stores vast.

Chronology begins with man !
But when did Earth begin ?
Time's chronicles had not began,
When Chaos enter'd in.

Man now begins to think and read,
T' examine and inquire
Into Life's purpose and his creed,
And thirsts for regions higher.

He finds himself a child of earth,
A pilgrim to the tomb ;
With few brief years betwixt his birth,
And Death's eclipsing doom !

The painful thought that he must die,
To him alone is giv'n :
Tho' it create a worldly sigh,
It wings his Soul to heav'n !

The hemisphere that bounds our ken,
Cuts every earthly tie :
But through death's screen Light shines again
On Immortality !

Hope's rainbow promise seems to say,
   The spirit never dies !
But after life shall pass away
   To its own native skies !

This elevates, resigns, inspires,
   And fills his grateful heart
With prayer and praise, and warm desires,
   To Heav'n ! when lov'd ones part.

Divinity is dew from Heav'n,
   An antidote for sin :—
A holy inspiration giv'n !—
   'The still small voice ' within.

Oh ! glorious mind that looks beyond
   The present changing scene
Of life's romantic journey round,
   And lives the two between !

Then when Death's solemn hour draws nigh,
   (Worn out on life's rough road,)
How peaceful to lie down and die ;
   Prepared to meet our God !

When round about our senses swim,
 And Earth recedes from view;
Th' expiring lamp of life grows dim,
 The soul is passing through!

Absorb'd, unconscious, in a trance,
 We sleep and wake no more!
Or waking take one parting glance,
 Of this world's fading shore!

Salvation is the soul set free,
 From cares and ills of life;—
Deliverance from captivity,
 Sin, sickness, sorrow, strife!

Theology! alas, thy schools
 Are factions,—full of strife!
All orthodox by logic rules,
 But heterodox in life.

The Catholic insidious rules
 The unenlighten'd crowd;
Anathemas and papal bulls
 Are hurl'd in thunders loud.

Their impious mummery is a sham,—
A scenic interlude :
With superstitions gross they cram
The ignorant multitude.

The Protestant, with kindred zeal,
His faith spreads far and wide ;
And both a rival interest feel,
Christ taking for their guide.

That cruel, false, and treacherous race,
The Jews ! th' elect of heaven ;
Whose doctrines christians half embrace,
Through earth are wanderers driven !

Mohammedans are zealots born ;
The Koran their belief !
Despising infidels with scorn,
Who worship not their Chief !

The simple Hindoos reverence pay
To all their household gods !
The Brahmin and the Buddhist pray
With special forms and modes.

The Pagans, primitive and rude,
   To Temple worship fly ;
With sacrifice themselves delude,
   And idol imagery !

Jehovah ! from his throne on high,
   On weak deluded man,
Looks down in pity with a sigh,
   At his frustrated plan.

Are things divine as we conceive ?
   Whose creed is wrong or right ?
We scarcely know what to believe,
   And need more spiritual light !

Belief or doctrine will not save
   The sinner from his fate :
We nothing know beyond the grave,
   But, hoping on, must wait.

Heroes and saints are deified
   Throughout the peopled earth ;
With bards divine who prophesied,
   And gods of monstrous birth.

Temples and groves and altars rose,
   And sacrifices made
With pious homage ; games and shows
   Lent ostentatious aid.

Church and Dissenters split, divide,
   The learned disagree :
Dogmatically all decide
   The old controversy.

Divorce the firm of Church and State,
   And plural livings drop ;
The mercenary sales abate,
   And base corruption stop.

In morals all mankind agree,
   And cordially unite !
Religion seems a mystery,
   For which fanatics fight.

With governments Religions change,
   For all think theirs the best !
Believing others false and strange,
   Each would destroy the rest.

Above all this my Soul aspires
    To search out Truth on high ;
Apart from doctrine it desires
    To feel Divinity !

Oh ! for that heav'n-felt spiritual glow,
    That fills the heart with love !
When our best feelings overflow,
    Soften'd by dews above !

Whatever spot of Earth we share,
    Has its establish'd creed ;
Which time and custom nourish'd there,
    And still preserves the seed.

Religion 's native to the breast,—
    Instinctive to our race :
With special forms each sect 's imprest,
    But *all* find equal grace.

The hopes and fears of future life,
    Influence our actions here ;
They tame our nature ;—crush our strife,
    And draw our Maker near.

What numbers worship in their zeal,
From superstitious fear
And ignorance! who never feel,
Or question what they hear!

Creatures of habit sent to school,
And trained to all that's taught ;
They learn Theology by rule,
Without a doubting thought.

To inbred dogmas man will cling,
Howe'er absurd and strange :
Opinion's a capricious thing !
Divine laws never change !

How whimsical the forms and modes
False piety inspires !
What bigotry in blood-writ codes
Blaze up the martyrs' fires !

Enough in natural laws is found,
T' illuminate the Mind !
The supernatural confound,
And mystify the blind !

How many thought in days of yore,
  This thought that still will rise ;
After deep search and pondering o'er,—
  That ' Truth in Nature lies !'

Simple and governed by one plan,
  Unchangeable ! divine !
The only book revealed to man ;—
  God's universal sign !

The Bible is the Word of God,
  The christian world believes !
The chart, the anchor, finger'd road
  To Heaven, which ne'er deceives.

Is it infallible or no ?
  Was every pen inspired ?
Does it reveal all man should know ?
  And all the world required ?

The Word of Life is everywhere,
  In nature and in man !
(Not partial creeds or books we share ;)
  An universal plan !

Growing intelligence will spurn,
   And science oft confute,
The instill'd doctrines which we learn,
   While understanding 's mute.

To blast and undermine the rock,
   On which the Bible stands,
Would echo like an earthquake's shock,
   Throughout all christian lands.

Investigation leads to doubt ;
   Doubt makes the sceptic pause,
Reflect, examine, reason out
   Of all things a First Cause !

Engraved upon the sage's mind,
   The shadow will not pass
For substance, though it cheat the blind,
   Unthinking, ignorant mass !

Entail'd opinions,—fixed belief,
   Are undermined and fall ;
Conventionalities are brief,
   Knowledge enlightens all !

The world 's fast waking from its dream !
   The Mind receiving light !
Darkness and superstition seem
   To blind the human sight.

The glorious light of Reason sheds
   Its rays on all around ;
Truth over falsehood reigns and spreads
   Her flowers where weeds abound.

The intellectual gift divine,
   In flashes first began,
Is now a glory made to shine
   And emblems God in man !

Were man to mark, learn and digest
   God's teachings in the heart ;
The anxious mind might be at rest
   He 's there reveal'd in part.

How melancholy 'tis to see.
   Such enmity and strife
In different sects, when such should be
   The bread and salt of life !

Alas ! unrighteous wars are bred,—
　Deluded millions die,
Martyrs to special faith, instead
　Of serving the Most High.

The holy wars we all deplore,
　For they were fought in vain :
What rivers flow'd with human gore !
　What hecatombs were slain !

If Heav'n appoints its missions here,
　'Tis proof of some great plan,
Which Providence will make appear,
　A blessing unto Man !

As oracles of truth and light,
　In characters divine,
Who bless'd the world with spiritual sight,
　Christ, Paul, and Moses shine !

Such pious guides we must admire,
　As ministers from Heav'n !
To lead, convert, and raise us higher,
　These righteous men were giv'n.

As other lights of wisdom shine,
   God's purpose to fulfil;
So these, as part of his design,
   Were agents of his Will.

Jesus ! the holiest of our race,
   The model we adore,
Preach'd moral truths we all embrace,
   And angels could no more !

This philanthropist of mankind,
   So holy, good, and pure,
Gave mental sight unto the blind,
   And Heaven to bless the poor.

The gospel is a song of joy,
   To those who Christ believe ;
But is there truth without alloy,
   And must we *all* receive ?

Of all religions we yet know,
   The Christian 's most divine
And spiritual ! a heaven below,
   Where all the virtues shine !

F

Another Saviour may arise,
  By Providence inspired!
To open up the inner skies,
  By all mankind desired!—

The harbinger of spiritual Light,
  About to shine on man!
Discerned by intellectual sight,
  Dim, distant, yet began!

When man, superior to our race,
  With giant strength of mind,
In later times shall take our place,
  And godlike wisdom find.

The shadow of a Faith appears,
  The whole world will embrace
Fraternally in after years,
  And all the rest displace.

The Universal church of God
  Is struggling into sight;
While doctrines of the past explode
  'Fore scientific light.

How many prodigies appear,
  To gem the world with light!
Distinguish'd in their natural sphere,
  Gifted with clair'vant sight!

All homage to th' illustrious great,
  Whose genius we admire!
The model men we imitate,
  Whose lofty works inspire!

Homer and Shakespeare still inspire,
  And thrill the soul within!
Plato and Socrates raise higher,
  And light divine let in.

As the world's teachers, and our guides,
  We honor, praise, esteem!
But to believe them Gods besides,
  Is impious, and a dream!

The great Eternal will not share
  His sov'reignty with man!
'Tis blasphemy in those who dare
  Plurality to plan!

Societies spread far and wide
    Their doctrines false or true,
And missionary work provide
    From their own points of view.

A dreamy phantom of the brain,
    The thing we Demon call ;
Vice, passion, crime, affliction, pain,
    Alas ! are bred in all.

Remote traditions, dreams obscure,
    Descend from sire to son ;
Myths, legends, miracles endure,
    And ghostly stories spun.

If the foundation is not sound,
    The edifice must fall :
Examine, search, and prove the ground,
    Before you build at all.

Uproot the fabric if corrupt,
    And Church and State reform ;
The reformation re-construct,
    Before the gathering storm.

'Twas quite as natural to die,
   As live before the fall !
Age brings decay ;—'tis destiny !
   Death ravenous swallows all !

In death we have no power to rise,
   The soul has pass'd away !
And tenantless the castle lies
   In ruin and decay.

To liberty mankind aspire !
   In free thought they delight !
Then why deprive the soul that's higher,
   Of intellectual light ?

To common sense we would appeal,
   And the unbiassed mind :
Not to the Jesuit's frantic zeal,
   So credulous and blind.

Instead of winning hearts by love,
   They'd govern all by fear !—
Would bring down vengeance from above,
   And shew no mercy here.

Church persecutions are a blot
   Of dark deluded times ;
Some tyrant king's or priesthood plot ;
   Inquisitorial crimes.

Religion, how we blush to hear
   Thy sacred name profaned,
By hypocrites, who would appear
   The monkish saints they feign'd.

Ignobly lowering God to man,
   With passions they inspire
The holy Spirit ! and would fan
   His anger into fire.

Revenge, hate, malice, jealousy,
   They impiously impute
To the all-loving Deity,
   As if a savage brute.

If we in miracles believe,
   And Nature's Laws suspend,
We supernatural powers conceive,
   But fail to comprehend.

Could Roman Priests absolve from sins,
 To them we'd daily fly ;—
Repent, confess with offerings,—
 Do penance, fast and die.

Such legends we cannot receive
 From pious saint or bard :
Enthusiasts themselves deceive,
 And truth with fiction lard.

Some visions look like mystic dreams,
 Poetical ! sublime !
With metaphor the language teems,
 O'er all the eastern clime.

The incantations of the night,
 Mysterious are to all ;
Revealing to our mental sight
 The preternatural !

But who will say they are divine
 Whisperings of God to man ?
The word, the oracle, the sign,
 To shadow forth his plan ?

Read, mark and learn ! seek God and truth,
   Take wisdom for thy guide ;
Think for thyself in age and youth,
   And let plain sense decide.

God publishes his wise decrees,
   Through the wide heavens and earth ;
Though man but indistinctly sees
   Their purpose, end, or birth !

The inspired oracles to man,
   Are written in his breast !
The decalogue with life began,
   But where are all the rest ?

War, incest, slavery, swearing, pride,
   Intemp'rance, lust, are crimes ;
Cheating, gambling, forgery, beside
   A host that stain our times.

The trials we here undergo,
   Which make our earth a hell ;
May be God's judgments here below,
   For aught that man can tell.

Can we perceive in this world's school
  A nursery for heaven ?
To weed out vice, and passions cool,
  And rectify the leav'n ?

What is our being's end and aim ?
  To propagate and die?
Or culture mind and nature tame,
  For all eternity ?

Delightful pleasure to possess
  Benevolence of heart ;—
To feel,—to mitigate distress,
  And charity impart !

Sisters of mercy, truth and love,
  Who worship and adore,
Receive their mission from above,
  To tend the sick and poor.

The zealous pastor all admire,
  Who comes the Soul to save ;—
To purify and raise it higher,
  And worthier Him who gave !

Let conscience regulate and steer,
  And virtue be our aim ;
They bring their own reward while here,
  And leave a deathless name !

Morality is worldly bliss,
  A blessing unto man !
Essential to a world like this,
  By criminals o'erran.

Apart from special doctrines taught,
  Who can indiff'rent be
To calm religious holy thought,
  And genuine piety.

The vital principle within
  A spark fans into flame,
And, like an antidote for sin,
  Our inbred passions tame.

Religion 's bliss to all our race,
  A glass we all look thro' ;
It brings our Maker face to face,
  And keeps our Heav'n in view.

It is the twilight of the soul,
  Catching a glimpse of heav'n ;
Attractive as th' magnetic pole,
  Or rock for safety driv'n.

Abstracted, prayerful and sincere,
  'Tis like a heav'n within ;
A peaceful calm and comfort here,
  With light divine let in !

In mellow age and sunset years,
  Its softening influence spreads
A tranquil smile o'er hopes and fears,
  With angels o'er our heads.

Exalted, spiritual, and sublime,
  It is a sacred tie
And covenant with God ! thro' time,
  And all eternity.

The pious soul, when snared in sin,
  To its Creator flies
For comfort and support within,
  In realms of ungauged skies.

This golden rule to all impart,
 ' Unite thyself to God
' With all thy soul, and mind, and heart,
 ' And walk His heav'nly road.'

To nobler being we aspire !
 A world of spiritual bliss !
Where thought will be exalted higher,
 Than it can reach in this.

Devotion elevates the Soul,
 Refines and draws us near
To Him who regulates the whole
 Of Being everywhere !

The Sabbath is a day of rest,
 From worldly toil set free,
With heav'nly aspirations blest,
 And sweet tranquillity.

Prayer is the heart's melodious strain,
 An anthem of the Soul ;
Its tones vibrate thro' every vein
 And nerve from pole to pole.

He who communes with God alone,
  In privacy retired,
And penitence before the throne
  Of Mercy, grows inspired!

The intellectual and refined
  High cultivation shew,
The spiritual and righteous mind
  Tastes Heav'nly bliss below!

Angelic beings here appear,
  And minds like jewels shine,
Belonging to a higher sphere,
  Celestial and divine!

Benevolence, and truth, and love,
  Are virtues which outshine;
And pious Faith, which points above,
  Is saint-like and divine!

Oh! give to me that spiritual light,
  Its influence let me feel!
Which Heav'n can open up to sight,
  And God himself reveal!

Teach me, my God ! thy paths to tread,
   And by thy compass steer ;
If I am heretic in head,
   My understanding clear !

As penitents we bow the knee,
   With reverence, faith and love ;
And pour out all our Soul to Thee,
   The great Unknown above !

THE FUTURE,

OR

SOUL, HEAVEN AND IMMORTALITY.

PART III.

The eternal shore—The Ghostly state—The spiritual world
—Purgatory—The Exiled Soul—Heaven—Creation's
works — Death — The released Spirit — Phantoms and
Shadows—Problem of the future State—Immortality—
The soul's pre-existent state—Eternity.

THE past's a picture half defaced !

   The present like a stream !

The future to which all things haste,

   An unrevealed dream.

Prophetic sybil ! now unfold

   Our destiny and fate !

Prepare my genius to behold,

   And sketch the shadowy state.

To look into the rolls of Time,
    Its secrets to discern ;
T' unveil the spiritual and sublime,
    Their mysteries to learn.

With preternatural sight inspire,
    And photograph my mind,
With views about which all inquire,
    And which th' immortal find.

Where Souls live in a conscious state
    Of blessedness and peace ;
Disfranchised from the world's estate,
    And Time's contracted lease.

Here let us bridge the gulf between
    Life and th' eternal shore !
And look across the ghostly scene
    Of spectres passing o'er.

As o'er the rainbow's arch they go,
    Their figures melt away :
Released from earth they onward flow
    In crowds the same highway.

The Earth recedes ; we slumbering lie
    Unconscious in a trance,
Dreaming of immortality,
    Of which we get a glance.

At a pavilion's entrance there,
    A priest in orders stood ;
Who scattered incense through the air
    From spice and sandal wood.

Th' ambrosial exhalations rose
    In clouds of rich perfume ;
O'erpowering with a drowsy doze
    Our senses with the fume. ,

Sight, scent, and hearing slowly fade,
    Like a dissolving view :
Stars, suns and moons sink into shade
    In firmament of blue.

Sweet dulcet sounds of music rise,
    Harmonious, soft, and clear,
Such as a saint hears when he dies
    When heralds wing'd appear ;

Blending their voices with the airs
    Celestial and divine ;
Mingling their symphonies and prayers,
    As they in concert join.

Through flowing robes of white attire,
    Transparent forms we see,
While the melodious lute and lyre
    Pour forth their minstrelsy.

Their graceful shadows glimmering past,
    Aerial, upward soar
To realms above, profound and vast,
    Beyond the ethery shore.

Legions of seraphs wing the skies,
    Arrayed in vestures white,
Inscrutable to mortal eyes,
    But clear to spiritual sight.

How playful fancy shifts the scene
    From this globe's bounded view !
And from behind peers through the screen,
    All curious to search through.

Oh ! for a sense of spiritual sight,
   Those regions to explore !
Illumined with ethereal light,
   And Heaven's bespangled floor.

Th' imaginative Future draws
   The distant landscape near ;
And o'er its imagery we pause,
   With glowing fancy here.

Those regions are a spectral state,
   On which the mind's eye feeds !
And speculative as our fate,
   In spite of worldly creeds.

A dream nocturnal,—unrevealed,—
   Unvisited,—unknown !
A foreign shore from sight concealed,
   Foreshadowed if not shewn.

We shape, build, theorize, decide,
   And image to our view :
But where's the chart and helm to guide
   Or soul to pierce them through ?

Exalted thoughts which elevate
　　The intellectual mind,
Come nearest to the spiritual state,
　　We shall hereafter find.

Philosophers of great renown,—
　　And priests who worked their spell,-
The visions of their minds have shewn !
　　But what can mortals tell ?

Were Bards inspired who touched the theme,
　　Original ! sublime !
Profane or sacred ! did they dream,
　　Of unbegotten Time ?

The master mind of Dante drew
　　Th' infernal shades to light !
And Milton's genius open threw
　　The gates of Paradise !

Shades of immortal men, arise,
　　Th' shadowy world foreshew !
Return to us in spectral guise ;
　　And unfold all ye know !

Illume our darkness and make clear
  Your destiny and state !
And if confined or free !—appear,
  And let us know our fate !

The oracles prognosticate,
  And prophecies proclaim,
The secrets of the Book of Fate,
  As if from Heaven they came.

Who can interpret things divine ?
  The spiritual reveal ?
Fathom the mysteries of design ;
  And break th' eternal seal ?

Astrologers consult the spheres,—
  Foretell our earthly fate :
Divines work on our hopes and fears,
  And sketch our future state !

An omen dark, foreboding ill,
  Is pictured in the sky !
A dream at night when all is still,
  Comes like a prophecy !

Where mountain chains close up the sky,
  A supernatural choir
Of voices issue from on high,
  And gradually expire.

Chain'd in oblivious bonds of sleep,
  Strange phantoms haunt us here ;
Aerial shapes and shadows deep,
  Emblem a spiritual sphere.

Is evil not personified,
  To work upon our fears ?
And our worst passions deified,
  By some infernal Peers ?

Have we a Genius at our side,
  A guardian angel dear ?
To counsel, influence, prompt and guide,
  Our wandering footsteps here ?

Magnetic influences attract,
  And kindred souls unite !
An unsolved problem, but a fact,
  To charm'd mesmeric sight.

The soul communion holds with soul,
 Though hemispheres may part:
And instant thought from pole to pole,
 Thrills through the human heart.

Let 's pause upon the Soul's estate,
 Worthy of thought sublime:
Its present life,—its future state!
 Eternity and Time!

What silly symbols of the Soul
 Imagination draws!
Reflective minds from pole to pole,
 Still o'er the problem pause.

Th' invisible we would explore,
 And draw aside the veil
That separates us from the shore
 Of shadows ghostly pale.

Shall there be held that great Assize,
 A general judgment day?
Or are we judged as each one dies,
 Can tawny sybil say?

In nether circles of the air,
  Are solitudes profound,
Where misery, suffering, and despair
  In dungeons deep abound.

Shall we for sins of Earth atone ?
  In living tombs abide ?
Will friends and relatives be known
  Across the Stygian tide ?

For sin, impiety and crime,
  There may be banishment
To shadowy regions for a time ;
  Not *endless* punishment :

Where guilty souls in anguish mourn
  Mid groans and awful cries,
By conscience, terror, torture worn,
  And lamentable sighs.

A dreary wilderness of wo,
  A desert, cavern, wood ;
Where evil spirits pine below
  In dismal solitude.

A place of horror, fear and pain,
　　Black, lonesome, silent, sad ;
Where gnawing conscience feeds again
　　On thoughts that drive them mad.

Dark, cheerless, desolate and cold,
　　A purgat'ry for sin ;
Where guilt and dread torment the bold,
　　And racking pains within.

Grief, toil, anxiety and care
　　Distract th' afflicted mind ;
And sting with madness and despair,
　　The lonely wretch confined.

Regret and sorrow for the past,
　　Will reach the ear of Heaven !
The most corrupt of Earth's outcast,
　　May hope to be forgiven !

The exiled Soul will reappear,
　　Reformed, regenerate, pure,
From realms of agony and fear,
　　And prisons that immure.

Transporting thought ! the spiritual clime,
   To which we all aspire ;
Celestial ! heavenly ! and sublime !
   Where reigns Creation's Sire !

The stars that gem the vaulted sky,
   A dense and glittering host,
To us unfold infinity,
   In endless mazes lost.

But what is Heaven ? that heav'n of love,
   A real and conscious state ?
A local dwelling-place above,
   Which prophet-bards create ?—

Perpetual sunshine ever cheers
   With gladness and delight,
The Soul released from mortal fears
   Of darkness, death and night.

Delicious odours fill the air
   Of this transparent clime ;
Where all is heavenly, bright and fair,
   Grand ! infinite ! sublime !

A world of purity and bliss,
  Where kindred spirits meet,
After a short sojourn in this,
  Their dearest friends to greet?

Where Eden's happiness is found,
  And peace serenely dwells;
Where harmony's in every sound,
  And not a thought rebels.

No anxious cares disturb the Soul,
  So tranquil, and serene!
No struggling passions to control,
  In that Elysian scene!

All that is beautiful to view,
  Or vision can create;
The good, the righteous, just and true,
  Will there illuminate

A nobler state of being,—new,
  On which we speculate,
And mirror to our ideal view;
  A theoretic state!

Robed in ethereal vestures white,
  The choir of Heaven appear,
With instruments reveal'd to sight,
  And vocal songsters there.

Where singing anthems to the throne
  Of Heaven's exalted King,
With chants of praise and worship crown
  Our fond imagining !

Oh ! for the better life beyond,
  Which brightens with its beams
The Soul like break of day when found
  After fantastic dreams.

Where soul communings are inspired,—
  And warmest feelings rise,—
Identity of mind acquired,
  In those transforming skies !

Our senses will be more acute,
  Our faculties refined ;
And memory take deeper root
  In Heaven's all-seeing mind.

Shall the appointed, vigils keep,
　　Each in their several spheres?—
In missions cross the skyey deep,
　　Commission'd by their peers?

How many heavens shall we ascend,
　　The topmost height to climb?
How long a period in each spend,
　　Ere reaching the sublime?

Shall we in holiness excel?
　　Perfection there attain?
Wisdom and knowledge store as well,
　　And fame unbounded gain?

Will brightest intellects below,
　　And genius most sublime,
Distinguish'd be,—and social grow,—
　　In that seraphic clime?

Shall the immortal great, whose fame
　　Was noised abroad through Earth,
Be known by instinct, like or name,
　　In this their spiritual birth?

Will graphic memory recall
　　The faded things of Time?
Will life's dramatic scenes at all,
　　Be mingled with sublime?

Shall souls revisit Earth again,
　　In spiritual disguise?
And o'er the grave cold corpse remain
　　To watch and sympathize?

Shall we progress? will knowledge charm,
　　As it expands the mind?
Shall we enjoy a sweeter calm?
　　And bliss of angels find?

The wonders of Creation fill
　　With admiration all!
But what discoveries will still
　　Attract beyond this ball?

The distant spheres to comprehend,
　　Examine and explore,
Will be our privilege, and tend
　　To make us thirst for more.

From knowledge new ideas will flow,
   Enlarge, exalt, and root,
For out of stems young branches grow,
   Bud, blossom, set, and fruit.

Possession will not damp desire,
   But relish stimulate
To further action, and inspire
   The soul to emulate.

There, souls of sentiment and song,
   And eloquence will meet ;
While some to festivals will throng,
   And some to calm retreat.

Perhaps, aspiring to excel,
   We shall the centre climb !
Until we reach the place where dwell
   Th' celestial and sublime !

Where dazzling rays of glory shine
   Resplendent round the throne !
Where sits th' Exalted Judge Divine !
   To whom all things are known !

Th' Holy of Holies there is found,
   Revealed to those forgiv'n :
Angelic beings there surround,
   With Hierarchy of Heav'n !

In circles thus Creation lies
   Developed to our view !
Where the aspiring spirit flies
   In quest of something new.

Philosophers and learned men,
   Their worldly knowledge gain
In the brief three score years and ten,
   Of life's extended chain.

If so much wisdom is acquired
   By intellectual Mind,
And dint of labour uninspired,
   What may we hope to find

In spiritualities sublime?
   And special influence?
Surpassed by all we know of time,
   Derived from natural sense?

The new, the glorious and unknown,
   Will be to us reveal'd ;
The infinite eternal shewn,
   And secrets here conceal'd.

The heavenly mansions of our rest,
   Pavilion'd courts above,
Are fill'd with spirits of the blest,
   All join'd in bonds of love.

Orders of angels,—spirits bright,
   And saints divinely fair,
Assembled round, will glad our sight
   With things all holy there !

With wreaths of glory round their head,
   And flowing robes divine,
They move with grace on wings outspread,
   And all illumined shine.

Rewards will differ in degree,
   For virtuous conduct here ;
Those who best serve the Deity
   Conspicuous will appear.

H

In dignity and robes of state,
   In countenance and tone,
Who on imperial Godhead wait,
   In glory round his throne.

Sense, faculties, and objects new
   Will there exalt the Mind,
Inheriting all it here knew,
   With all it longs to find !

The rays of gladness and delight
   Will fill our souls above
With wisdom's intellectual light
   And pure seraphic love.

Choice harps and lutes of richest tone,
   And harmony divine,
Fill heaven's melodious courts and throne,
   Where suns perpetual shine !

Ethereal treasures ! heavenly calm,
   The haven of our rest ;
Thou hast within a healing balm,
   For every troubled breast.

A foretaste of that heav'n above
  Is realized below,
By those who 're extasied with love
  And feel a rapturous glow.

If small things may with great compare,
  'Tween this world and the next,
What myriads will be gather'd there,
  Should all worlds be annexed !

All who inhabited afar,
  The globes that stud the sky,
In farthest nebulæ or star,
  Will meet their God on high !

What swarms of beings crowd the scene
  Of our industrious hive !
Whole generations pass unseen !
  Yet millions more survive !

Life's drama must be acted through,
  And each one take a part
Upon the stage, his work to do,
  Ere he this scene depart !

When Death's dissolving hour draws nigh,
 And leaves of autumn fall;
'Tis our translation to the sky;
 A passport given to all.

Into Death's valley we descend,
 The world recedes from view;
Heaven opens o'er us, we ascend
 To prospects wide and new.

Released from bonds the Spirit flies,
 In wandering mazes lost!
Doubtful it navigates the skies,
 By sportive breezes tost.

Like an imprison'd bird set free,
 It pants with wild delight,
In phrensy and with ecstasy,
 And soft ethereal light!

Pent up in alabaster shrine,
 While pilgriming the Earth;
The twinkling stars too dazzling shine,
 Launched forth to its new birth.

From star to star it swiftly flies,
   An alien from its home ;
And half the firmament descries
   Beneath the spacious dome.

Until some fleet wing'd seraphs see,
   In starlit spaces lost,
The wandering exiled refugee,
   And guide it to its post.

As gravitation to the Sun
   Is one of nature's laws ;
The Soul, when its career is run,
   To central Godhead draws.

Hope beckons us through yonder skies,
   Where Faith has fix'd her home ;
There our pictorial visions rise,
   Of heav'nly joys to come !

Yet destiny is so obscure,—
   The future so profound
And reachless, we deem nothing sure
   Beyond this planet's bound.

Where are our friends who 've gone before,
   The great,—the good,—the wise ?
What influence guides? what loadstone shore
   Attracts within the skies ?

Phantoms and shadows fan the air,
   Invisible as wind ;
Wand'ring instinctively to share
   Th' electric spark of mind.

The whispering breezes round us play,
   Laden with rich perfume ;
Meeting and fluttering on their way,
   Aerial shapes assume.

The breath of heaven they seem to bring ;—
   Are musically sweet ;—
And playful as the gladdening Spring,
   Which comes with smiles to greet.

These may be friends in spiritual guise,
   Whose sympathy and love,
Though undiscern'd by mortal eyes,
   Attracted from above.

Their hallowed memories flit before
  The visionary mind,
Whose latent faculties restore
  And reproduce our kind !

They walk in secret, veiled in light
  Of gossamer around ;
Pale spectral forms, half hid from sight,
  In lonely regions found !

Is that an apparition bright,
  That speeds o'er land and sea,
Communicating in the night
  A friend's death instantly ?

Delusive phantoms of the mind,
  The imagery of thought,
The curtain'd scenic views behind,
  By fertile genius wrought.

Till death we must with patience wait,
  These problems to unfold ;
And what shall be our after state,
  By bards in visions told.

Then the great secret will be known,
    And Truth and Light appear ;
Discoveries there will be our own,
    We tried to find out here.

Each one a character unfolds,
    Distinct from all the rest ;
By Nature cast in different moulds,
    And in their souls imprest.

Oh ! withering thought, when all is o'er,
    To perish when we die !
Annihilation ?—live no more ?—
    A blank Eternity ?—

That all we see, admire and love,
    Will like the flow'rets fade ?
Utopian dreams of heav'n above,
    Sink into sunless shade ?

Oblivion is a state of death,
    Like to unconscious sleep
Without revival, motion, breath ;
    Dark, viewless, senseless, deep !

Mankind will build their hopes on high,
   Delusive though it be!—
Believe in a futurity,
   And in the Soul set free!

The disembodied Soul will rise
   To its Creator there,
Through brilliant shining jewel'd skies,
   And soft ambrosial air.

The hope of Immortality
   Revives the spirit here;
For though its twin companion die,
   The Soul will reappear!

Our onward destiny and doom
   A secret must remain:
'Tis vain presumption to assume;
   We hope to live again!

In this mankind are all agreed,
   It suits their wishes best;
However opposite their creed,
   It animates the breast.

Till Life's dream shall have passed away,
　We'll place our trust in God ;
With reverence worship and obey,
　While journeying on the road.

Hope cheers us with her smiling face,
　And angel brightness there !
Imagines a superior place,
　To this we mortals share !

We have enshrined within the breast,—
　Creative brain, and eye,—
The noblest,—most exalted test,
　Of our Divinity !

When half the world lies in a trance,
　And visions haunt the mind,
Unconsciously we get a glance
　Of shadowy realms behind.

The gentle, light and graceful shades,
　Who timidly retire,
Were once the sweet and lovely maids,
　Whose magic charms inspire.

Whose feminine attractions melt
   The coldest, proudest heart ;
Whose influence and dominion 's felt
   In every counterpart.

Their symbols, like the painter's art,
   Embody forth to view
The scenes in which they take their part,
   Creations grand and new !

Pale spectres flit about the air,—
   In groups assemble round,
And sweet communion seem to share,
   In bowers of bliss profound.

Dim figures of the living type,
   Transparent, fill the scene :
Babes, youths, the middle aged and ripe,
   Are chang'd from what they 'd been.

All active and in motion seem,
   On some great errand bent ;
Invisible and like a dream,
   Each on its mission sent.

The resurrection of the dead
   Is but a myth we share!
The mortal parts dissolve and spread
   In vapours through the air.

The glorified and vital spark
   Soars on expanded wings,
And like the heaven descending lark,
   Midway its carol sings.

Oh! let us more familiar grow
   With our Immortal part!
Ethereal essence, Thee I'd know!
   Oh! teach me what thou art!

Great luminary of the mind,
   Of intellectual light!
I'm curious to search out and find
   Thy origin and flight!

Thy sphere and birth?—primeval state?
   Thy wand'rings to and fro?
Thy antecedents,—future fate?
   And change to undergo?

Mysterious, flick'ring, shadowy thing !
   What is thy mission, pray ?
Thou art but briefly tenanting
   This mansion-house of clay.

To think, feel, hope, reflect, aspire,
   Are attributes divine !
Which rank thee in creation higher
   Than this transparent shrine !

Oh ! wilt thou in a conscious state,
   From crucible refined,
With other gentle spirits mate ?
   And divine favour find ?

Hast thou remembrance of the past,
   The interior world to shew ?
Where fate and destiny are cast,
   And laws of nature flow ?

Does life beyond resemble this,
   When mind and heart are pure ?
Is it that paradise of bliss
   Of which we make so sure ?

Not unremembered shalt thou go,
　　But leave a deathless name
Behind thee, if thou 'lt wiser grow,
　　And seek immortal fame.

Not undistinguish'd wilt thou be,
　　In heavenly courts above,
If thy works here are worthy thee,
　　And the great God of love!

Incarnate traveller!—restless guest!
　　Gifted with memory, tell
Thy former state and place of rest,—
　　And star where thou didst dwell?

We know that thou wilt pass away,—
　　This solid crust must die;
And all sublunary things decay!
　　But thou 'rt a mystery!

How oft we theorize and view,
　　In speculations lost,
Thy lineage, like, ethereal hue,
　　And what resemblest most!

Through intellect the soul doth shine,
   In eloquence of tongue ;—
In imagery and light divine,
   And all inspiring song.

It mantles in the glowing cheek,
   And flashes in the eye ;
In conscience it is heard to speak,
   And through our senses sigh.

To fancy, recreate, and feel
   The high poetic vein
Of imagery around us steal,
   Is music to the brain.

Our sentimental thoughts will rise
   Above this vale of tears ;
And spring to more congenial skies,
   And brighter, happier spheres !

Doubts and perplexities surround,
   As clouds obscure the light ;
For truth, like gold, is often found
   In depths beyond our sight.

We cannot penetrate the veil
  That hides our future fate ;
But without chart or compass, sail
  Life's ever changing state.

The vital spark returns to heaven,—
  In God it puts its trust ;
And if in exile here 'tis driv'n,
  Who doubts the sentence just ?

It ranges through infinity,
  In tortuous mazes lost ;
Spectator of eternity,—
  A pre-existent ghost !

Oh ! what a change to undergo,
  The soul from bonds set free !
It almost puts one in a glow,
  'Tis such felicity !

Ah ! how we love to ruminate,
  And on the future draw !
Forecasting our hereafter state,
  With sight oracular !

Th' eternal regions, how profound !
   A sea without a shore !
Space dotted with the globes around !
   And unseen millions more !

Eternity ! thou 'rt everywhere ;
   All other things have place ;—
The sea, the sun, and every sphere ;
   But thou art lost in Space !

The infinite above,—below,
   Without a centre,—height
Or limit to which thought might go,
   Or links of chain unite !

The source ! the fountain ! and the head,
   Who ? whence ? and how produced ?
Whose essence through all things is spread,
   And Providence diffused !

A living miracle, which mind
   Can't comprehend or reach !
The infinite and undefined
   Intelligence all preach !

The Past has vanished like a dream !

 The Present still flows on !

The Future, like a mirage stream,

 Recedes, and draws us on !

TIME AND ETERNITY.

The tie is broken : soul and body part,
For Death dissolves their union here at last,
After a rapid journey o'er the stage
Of active life ! and the enchanting spell
Of this world's busy scenes has pass'd away !
The tenant of that chamber is no more,
Where all is dark and silent as the tomb !

Thus one by one we're snatch'd from off the earth
We live on, tracking the steps of those
Who pass'd before us on the stage of Time ;
Succumbing to the fate allotted all
Without distinction ! sparing neither sex,
The leaf of Autumn, or the flower of Spring,
Nor wealth which could afford to purchase life,
Nor ties that twine around the human heart,
Nor worth and goodness which we ill can spare,

Nor genius sublime, or wisdom deep!
All! all! this debt of nature soon must pay,
Some in the morn, the noon, the eve of life,
Making their exit many kind of ways!

So hath it ever been from time remote!
The past, the shadow of the things that were,
Succeeded and perpetuated by
The fleeting present! ever on the wing
And by the rising generation will
Be called the past! Thus youth creeps on to age
Throughout the feverish term of anxious life,
Revealing the dark future, which is near,
Deep and unfathomable as the void
We see above us, which we cannot gauge!

Time measured is, its boundary we define,
In circling periods of days and years,
And trace its progress from the birth of Man;
Th' events of which are briefly chronicled
In history's diary, while the world was young,
And heaven held intercourse with fav'rite man!
While Nature's cheerful face was lit with smiles
Of summer sweetness and inspiring rays,

Imparting blessings to the fruitful earth,
Green, flowery, full of promise, budding forth !

Ages have roll'd, but not in silence pass'd !
Nations of eminence been swept away !
And conquering heroes, powerful in their day,
Lie like their prostrate empires in the dust ;
The sad memorials of an Age remote !
Egypt, Assyria, Persia, where are ye ?
Greece, Rome, Judea, Carthage, Palestine !
Whose scatter'd ruins shew were once they stood.
War, conquest, age, have left them solitudes !
While countless numbers famous in their hour,
Are lost for ever in the lapse of Time,
Trod under and their names quite blotted out !

So perish all ! the world is full of change ;
The powerful wither, and the weak arise
To dignity and station by their deeds ;
And for a season lord it o'er the earth ;
Then plunge like meteors down oblivion's gulf !
The inquiring Traveller visits oft the spots
Which fame has consecrated, and the tombs
Held sacred for their antiquarian dust,

Of warriors, poets, statesmen, patriots, kings,
Philosophers and others of renown,
While breathing o'er their ashes in deep thought
Absorbed! transported into distant times;
Growing familiar with the things that were,
But passing not the barrier of the grave!

Oh! for some magic lamp! some genii's power!
Some supernatural agent to foreshew
And work a miracle,—to shadow forth
And picture the creations of a mind,
Soaring poetical on fancy's wing;
The invisible and future to unfold!
And draw the curtain of the spectral world,
That we might witness all that's passing there!
Could this enchanting scene be conjured up,
Then might the intellectual mind's-eye view,
And recognise the shades of those we knew!
The dear companion and the bosom friend,
Whose social intercourse illumed the hour,
While pilgrims passing through this lower sphere!

Have souls unbodied any thought of Earth?
Do they revisit it and sympathize

With those they were familiar with before !
Or are they doing penance for their sins
Committed here, before they can ascend
The highest heav'n to join the immortal throng ?
And mix with holy angels bright and pure,
Where spiritual felicity abounds,
With innocence and loftiness of thought,
And bliss celestial mortals dream not of !

Oh ! what a world of intellectual light,—
Of love and happiness should we behold
Assembled there in their seraphic charms !
Immortal, bless'd, united, equal all,
The family of Deity itself !
Where virtue is triumphant !—love divine !—
Truth ever sacred !—piety sincere !—
Sweetness with elegance and grace combin'd,
And all that here ennobles and endears
Mankind to man,—all that we praise, admire
And love of goodness is exalted there !
The generous of heart, and noble mind,—
The amiable, the pious, good and kind,—
And wisdom with her oracles of truth !
And prophet bards inspired ; and nature's sons,

With classic orators of flowery speech,
And philosophic sage well read and learn'd,
Stripped of all human passions,—thoughts corrupt,-
Degenerate vices,—base and sordid views,—
And the long catalogue of mortal ills,
And human frailties which afflict the earth !

MONODY.

As when a cloud o'erhangs the mountain's brow,
Its shadow flings and darkens all below;
So doth th' insatiate avarice of the Tomb
O'er sunbright spirits cast a mournful gloom;
When those we loved and honoured, and held dear,
Are summon'd hence, and from us disappear!
Not he who leaves his father-land to go
To climes beyond the sea he does not know
(Though friend or brother), when his home departs,
Will so depress our full,—our breaking hearts:
The emigrant can write, and we may hear!
The dead are silent through the circling year!

Our bliss suspended, and our serious air,
Our pensive thoughts, and visage hung with care,
Our restless spirits in their cells confin'd,—
Our mental sickness, and our absent mind,—

Our inward feelings, and our outward guise,
Bespeak a sorrow deeper than the eyes !
Indiff'rent to the world, dejected, still,
Absorbed ! reflective ! melancholy ! ill !

How measureless our steps are to the grave !
How brief the journey to the martial brave !
Alas ! when lengthened to its widest span,
How short the thread of life allow'd to man !
But yesterday (so swift-wing'd Time appears)
He we lament, though in the vale of years,
In health sat smiling in his easy chair,
A patriarch amidst the young and fair :
The jocund laugh, the rapt'rous kiss went around,
And he amongst the Christmas sports was found.
The spirit-stirring tale,—harmonious song,
With social discourse cheer'd the hours along.
All cheerful, patient, humble, frank, and plain,
His face was index of his musing brain,
Ennobling virtues of the wise and great,
Inspired his soul the best to emulate.
His disposition affable and mild,
Diffused a cheerfulness, and gladness smiled
Around like summer's rays diffusing joy,

When man feels all the transport of the boy.
Reason's bright lamp illumed his virtuous soul,
And kept the latent passions in control.
No angry feeling lurk'd within his breast,
No inward monitor disturbed his rest.
The voice of pity reached his tender heart,
And nature triumphed over selfish art :
Distress found sympathy, and age a friend,
To each would he some words of comfort send :
He sought to heal the wounds he could not cure,
And soften down the miseries of the poor.

As to the summer's day succeeds the night,
Whose long drawn shadows curtain up heav'n's light,
And shuts the glorious landscape from our sight ;
So to our dazzling eye and sunbright face,
Our sparkling spirits, happy dwelling-place,
Our smoothly gliding life and tranquil breast,
Succeed the sorrows of our souls distressed.
The flickering hope which glisten'd in the eye,
Like the arched iris of the stormy sky,
Which flatter'd and beguiled, though mixed with fears,
Ceased to illumine and left all in tears.
The link which chain'd his mortal part to earth,

Has passed the boundaries of its second birth :
And unencumber'd of its mortal load,
In heav'n appears with angels round its God !
As the rude tempest or autumnal breeze
Sweeps off in showers the foliage of the trees,
So nips the withering blight from off the stage
The wintry honours of a ripe old age.

If melting sorrow and pathetic grief,
Can in mute loneliness afford relief,
While pining o'er his tombstone, it is this,—
The mourn'd, the lov'd, dwells in the realms of bliss !
We in oblivion bury every fault,
The good alone rememb'ring of the past.
Speak of his virtues, and with gladness hear
All that's familiar and to memory dear.
Admire his maxims and whate'er was great,
Dwell on his proverbs and his tales relate !
But chiefly we recite beyond the rest,
His dying words engraven in the breast.

So meteor like and rapid was his flight
From earthly regions to the realms of light ;
So recently in festive scenes we met,

'Tis like a dream to think his sun has set.
Reflected in our fancy he appears,
In all the mellowness of riper years ;
When Time's invasions round his fabric spread,
And mowed the honours of his snow-white head.

Experience tells how hard it is to part,
With the dear treasures of a loving heart ;
How sacred relics of departed time !
How treasured antiques of a foreign clime !
When curious cabinets their stores unfold,
How many time-worn fragments we behold,
Preserv'd in coats of sacred mould or rust ;
Remains of nations prostrate in the dust !
If such their worth in antiquarian eyes,
Much more should be the gift of friends we prize.
Those friends removed, though trifle 'twas before,
A keepsake is, and trifle is no more :
Time sanctifies,—its value will increase,
And sacred 'twill be held till our decease.
Say should the portrait of a friend appear,
To raise emotions and to draw a tear,
Where we can every living feature trace,
With thoughts which dawned through his reflective face

And reading eye; how valuable the boon,
With which instinctively our hearts commune:
Which brings the dead to mind,—revives the past,
Ere life's fresh bloom by sickness was o'ercast.

While pondering thus, our memory reviews
A much lov'd parent through the sorrowing Muse;
May we in actions emulate our sire,
And imitate the virtues we admire:
Like him, our thoughts 'twixt heaven and earth divide,
And in an all-wise Providence confide!
May pious actions and inspiring prayer,
The mortal for th' immortal state prepare;
That when the ethereal spirit leaves behind
Its tenantless abode, we may be join'd
With those who shared our friendship and our love,
While passing thro' this world to that above.
May we ne'er try his memory to efface,
But in our musing bring him face to face.
Withdrawing from the world in pensive gloom,
We'll visit oft the ashes of his tomb;
In tenderness bedew them with our tears,
While th' immortals watch from yonder spheres!

IN MEMORIAM.

SHE like a broken column rent in twain
Mourns o'er the sacred spot where he was lain,
Brooding upon the memories of the past,
Afflicted, sorrowful, and overcast.
Her broken spirit, and her contrite heart,
Shew'd that with life and empire she could part,
Now the dear Prince who shared her nuptial bed,
Grasp'd in the iron hands of Death lay dead!

No sympathy of feeling can console
The deep emotions of her trembling soul;
The world cannot seduce, nor time efface
The index of that melancholy face,
Once lit with sunny smiles, whose lustre shed
The rays of glory round her wreath-crown'd head.
The nation joins its sorrows with her own,
In fond remembrance, and pathetic tone,
Her loss bewailing with its generous tears,

While offering up to Heav'n its earnest prayers
For since her people have his praises sung,
And his rare virtues hang on every tongue,
Connecting charities with Albert's name,
And exhibitions with his world-wide fame,
His worth and goodness burst into a blaze
Of glorious sunshine and immortal praise,
When his last sunset closed upon the scene,
And then reveal'd the past of what he 'd been ;—
A guardian angel of th' imperial crown,
Whose counsel ruled the empire and the throne.

What would we give could we our friends restore,
And be to them all we had been before ?—
United, happy, loving, faithful, true,
With heaven below and paradise in view !
Conscience reproaches us when we reflect
Upon the hasty word, or cold neglect ;
We lavish praises on the missing dead,
And o'er their ashes streams of sorrow shed,
Then on the tomb inscribe the tender line,
' In Memory' of those for whom we pine,—
With wreaths immortal sanctify the ground,
And strew fresh flowers upon the little mound ;

Then raise a mausoleum to their fame,
Adorn'd with garlands round their honour'd name.

We visit oft the hallowed spot held dear,
And consecrate it with a silent tear,
Reviving the remembrance of the past,
And solemn death-sleep when we watch'd his last.
Absorb'd in thought and musing o'er his tomb,
We pause upon the universal doom,
And feel that we must soon or later share
The common lot which ends this world of care.

To silvan shady groves would she retire,
T' indulge her grief in mourning's black attire,
Pour out her soul in lamentations loud,
And shun the notice of the vulgar crowd,
To find that solace which the world can't give.
And in the paths of heaven and virtue live.
The crimson tint has left her hollow cheek,
And she is humbled to the dust, and meek ;
Though once high-spirited and proud withal,
She is subdued, and pride has had its fall.
Paternal love and fondness intertwine,
Like the embracing tendrils of the vine,

K

The weaker branches clinging to the strong,
Which nourish and support the frail and young;
Where th' affections tenderly unite,
And joys Elysian gladden and delight.
His darling children he appeared to rule,
But play'd and frolick'd with them out of school;
His thoughts were imaged in his earnest look,
And they his prudent counsel always took :
The works he cherished, and the books he read,
Will be remembered with the things he said.
How doubly charming will appear to view,
This work of art, and *that* his fancy drew;
The treasured relics which he most admired,
Shew taste refined and knowledge well-acquired;
But chiefly one attracted her fond gaze,
And such a portrait merited her praise,
So like in features, semblance, grace, and dress,
It seemed his thoughts and actions to express!

Mother of princes, whose ancestral line
In ancient records eminently shine,
Whose wide dominions stretch beyond the sea,
The compass round of all geography :
Receive a people's homage and regards,

Of inspir'd orators and Attic bards,
Who with one heart thy widowhood deplore,
And sigh to think thy Albert is no more !
The Constitution claims thee for its own,
With Lords and Commons circled round thy throne ;
Admired and loved wherever known or seen,
A pattern mother, and a model Queen !
Thy progeny, now fatherless and young,
Who from the happiest of unions sprung,
Demand protection, and thy care require,
Depriv'd of the example of their sire,
To guide, instruct, inspire them what to do,
This vice to strangle, and that good pursue ;
And last not least, religion to instil,
To curb their tempers and rebellious will !

HOME.

WHEN the shadowy wings of evening enfold the orb of day,
And the nightingale is singing in the copse her
  sprightly lay,
How sweet it is to wander by the clear meandering
  stream,
Lit by the struggling moonbeams and the glowworm's
  starry gleam.

The softly flowing rivulet that's warbling at our feet,
Recalls to memory the voice of one so loved and sweet,
Which like the tuneful echoes of the distant village
  chimes,
Revives those thrilling ecstacies we felt in early times.

As we grow the streams of life into other channels flow,
Where struggling with the swelling deep and raging
  winds that blow,
Like the hapless maid whose bosom into little billows
  swells,

We anchor on the past o'er which remembrance
fondly dwells.

Thus the scenes of our childhood pass in panoramic view,
And youth and its connexions with a crowd of friends
ensue,
And though absence long has weaned us from the
old paternal dome,
If our fancies don't deceive us there's no spot like
that of home.

There we recognize the tree haply planted at our birth,
The venerable church, drilling school, and social hearth ;
But above these chronicles of youth, our sire in his arm
chair,
With his snowy locks and wintry looks sits like a
Druid there.

Oh ! how oft his heart has sung, and his face been lit
with joy,
When praises have been showered upon his dear, his
hopeful boy,
While through this picture of himself he images a race,
Inheriting his honoured name and lineaments of face.

But oh ! on our revisiting, how moving 'tis to hear
The voice which sung the lullaby so sweetly in our ear,
And with a mother's love to enrapture us with blisses,
Imprinted on our infant lips her sweetest, warmest
    kisses.

While watching o'er our slumbers then and filled with
    tender feeling,
In silent thought how many tears would through her
    eyes be stealing ;
How many a throb her heart would fetch, when
    picturing in her mind
Our future history which she like an oracle divined !

If pure affection ever dimm'd with tears a sister's eye.
When we have stood upon the brink of dark eternity,
How absence will endear us to each other when we
    meet,
Where love and sympathy have caused our kindred
    hearts to beat.

If to Friendship, Love, and Truth, we our sorrows
    would impart,
We seek to enshrine them in a virtuous woman's heart ;

And where can we hope to find, if we look the wide
    world through,
A heart more kind and feeling than a mother's that
    beats true ?

How feelingly the emigrant will mirror in his mind
The dear companions of his youth whom he hath left
    behind !
In pensive mood how oft will seek the grove or winding
    stream,
And of his past, his home, his friends, indulge a
    pictured dream !

THE WEDDING.

THE auspicious smiles of heaven welcome in the
    nuptial day,
And scented thorns and lilacs sweeten all the break of
    May ;
The laburnum's ringlets flowing like a rocket's sparks
    on high,
Look like a shower of firework stars descending from
    the sky.

Morning breaks the gates of slumber, and the chamber
    of the fair
Opens to the blooming bridesmaids who attend her
    toilet there :
While the tuneful village bells from yon ivy-mantled
    tower,
Proclaim the joyful tidings of the happy bridal hour.

Now in stately equipage comes the timid lovely bride,
With a pretty group of nymphs in white satin by her
    side ;
Her countenance is veiled like a rose in silver dew,
Whose modesty unfolds its blush of innocence to view.

To the village church in state the invited guests repair,
And meet encircled by his friends the hopeful bride-
    groom there :
Through a silvan grove of trees lined with gossips smart
    but poor,
Who strew the path with choicest flowers, she enters
    Hymen's door.

All that 's fair in heaven or earth that can captivate
    the heart,
The beautiful of nature and the elegant of art,
Adorn the timid maiden as she passes up the aisle,
Met with the warmest welcome and an all-inspiring
    smile.

They met like familiar friends who 've not been long
    apart,
With affection's smiles of love and with o'erflowing
    heart :

Their spirits sink into their breasts which quicken with
    deep feeling,
And through the maid's transparent cheek the crimson
    clouds are stealing.

The richest silks of India, with the jewels of Peru,
Vie with her clust'ring ringlets, and her languid eye of
    blue :
The expression of her countenance effeminately mild,
And she comes as if from heaven to tame and cultivate
    the wild.

Before the sacred altar, with their bosom friends around,
They plight their troth together and in wedding chains
    are bound,
How beautiful the virgin blushes hang upon the tree !
How like a saint of heaven she looks upon her bending
    knee !

Here the pledges of affection which all true lovers bind
Are redeemed with the promises late emblem'd in the
    mind ;
The tutelary father gives away the charming bride,
As she agitated stands close by her adorer's side.

The bridegroom takes his wife with a tremulous emotion,
And the bride looks on her husband with a confident
    devotion ;
Her looks are looks of tenderness, and his noble and
    sincere,
He struggles with his feelings, and she stems the
    pearly tear.

In token of his sacred vows he weds her with a ring,
Her heart speaks through her quivering lips, as she
    covenants to cling,
In sickness, health, and fortune, or adversity's fell stroke,
To the idol of her heart, like the ivy to the oak.

Through the passages of life, till our pilgrimage is o'er,
How many of its incidents are dated from this hour !
When two congenial spirits, wandering like the stars
    above,
Gravitate towards each other and are linked in bonds
    of love.

TO ONE IN A DECLINE.

"Forget" thee ! oh, no never, while the lamp of life will
    burn,
And that which had existence will through memory
    return :
The dazzling world may spread its snares, and I
    entangled be,
But my wandering thoughts will ever and anon return
    to thee.

There's nothing in thy maiden bloom that I could
    wish to blot,
But still if thou hast blemishes, by me they're all
    forgot.
May I live and die like thee,—"hear, kind Heaven, my
    earnest prayer !"
And possess those heavenly virtues which will be thy
    passport there.

I have seen the rainbow tints in thy countenance at
play,
I have watched the fairest flower in thy soft cheek
fade away ;
And drooping as thou sat'st, with thy clustering ringlets
bending,
I have seen the pearly shower in thy snowy breast
descending.

From those coral lips of love sweetest gems of fancy
sprung,
But now only whispers float from thy melodious tongue.
That sparkling soul which shone so bright in thy
resplendent eye,
Waned like the moon and vanished like that torch
from out the sky.

Beneath the weeping willow that o'erhangs the limpid
stream,
Sequestered in thy loneliness, how saint-like didst
thou seem,
When I have seen thee musing, as the sun was fast
declining,
On an unseen world beyond us with rays of glory shining.

If devotion can endear, or o'erflow the heart with
    feeling,
It will before her God to see a lovely woman kneeling !
Thy vigils have been constant at the hallowed hour of
    nine,
For through thy chamber's lattice we have seen the
    taper shine.

Sweetest minstrel of the lyre ! are thy inspirations o'er?
Shall we hear the muses weep in thy elegies no more ?
Will the embers of thy genius with thyself consume
    away ?
Will our feelings like a river swell o'er thy pathetic lay ?

It clouds the mind to see thee, Ellen, sickening in thy
    prime,
And separating from the world, alas ! before thy time :
'Tis painful to behold the rose-bud wither on the tree,
But melancholy to behold the blight of death on thee !

A VALENTINE.

LIKE comets wandering through the sky,
   Amid the solar systems free,
About this nether world we fly
   On pinions of full liberty;
Till destiny directs our flight,
   And then like doves on the same bough,
In search of pleasure we alight,
   And feel our heart's blood warmer flow.
With one consent the feathered pair
   Receive each other's fond addresses,
And to their bridal nest repair,
   Filled with affectionate caresses.
Oh! could I thus be wed to thee,
   I freely would my all resign,—
Forego unfettered liberty,
   To league my destiny with thine,
              My Valentine!

THE CLOSING SCENE.

Fast sinking in the sleep of death,
Ere ebbing life resign'd its breath,
He woke as if from dreams sublime,
As he cross'd o'er the bridge of Time ;
To take one parting, last adieu,
Of Earth receding from his view !

He fix'd his spirit-speaking eye
On his dear friends assembled nigh,
Absorbed and watching by his side,
In solemn silence as he died !
That thoughtful look showed more of mind,
Than thoughts outspoke by half mankind !

It was an index to his breast,
Which told of peace and heav'nly rest ;
And seemed to say with smile of love,—

" How beautiful shines all above !
A new Creation seems to rise
Beyond th' illuminated skies !

" Half mortal ! half immortal too !
On the world's edge, I 've heaven in view ;
Wing'd Seraphs whisper,—' Haste away,'
While distant music cheers the way :
My mind 's confused,—my eyes grow dim,
And round about my senses swim.

" Sylph-like forms,—aerial graces,
Phantoms look of angel faces ;
The magical illusions seem
Enchantment's spell !—or fairy's dream !
And fancy so bewilders me,
I feel I must a spirit be !"

Oh ! for some occult art to find
Entrance to his pictorial mind !
That all these grand enchanting views
Of th' inner world, we might not lose !
A foresight thus to mortals giv'n,
Would surely win their souls to heaven !

L

The Soul rush'd full into his eyes,
  Transient scenes but to survey ;
Then springing to its native skies,
  Left the warm expiring clay !
Thus these twin companions sever,
When his blue eye closed for ever !

Still the pulse is slowly beating ;
  Gently dies the breath away ;
Life itself is fast retreating ;
  Darkness clouds the face of day ;
O'er him steals the marble coldness,
Now his mortal part is soulless !

The great Secret 's now discovered,
  Which through life remained conceal'd ;
Doubts and fears dispersed, which hover'd,
  And th' invisible reveal'd !
Death ! Death alone presents the key
And shows our future destiny !

If that tranquil sleep is dying,
Dreaded Death is not so trying,
As is Life with sickness shrouded,

Fill'd with wants,—with miseries crowded !
'Tis in parting friends feel sorrow,
For they meet not on the morrow !

A generation swept away,
Proves all are hast'ning to decay ;
The past reflected but reveals
How swift-wing'd Time o'er all things steals,—
That we 're but travellers on the road.
And Life encumbered with a load.

THE BLIGHTED BLOSSOM.

Like the flickering lamp that fades
In its crystal shrine that shades,
Is the soul that dimly shineth,
When its mortal part declineth.

The slow disease wastes her away
Into a shadow day by day;
The form and features of her face,
So altered, we can scarcely trace.

The teasing cough,—perspiring frame,--
The crimson flush, and inward flame,
Show dissolution to be near,
And from us draw affection's tear.

To-day her health and spirits rise,
How large and bright her glassy eyes!
Alternate hope and timid fear,
Raise and deject while lingering here.

The clammy hand and stifling breath,
Are signs of her approaching death ;
And sleep, the nurse of every kind,
Steals o'er her calm unconscious mind.

The plaintive whisper travels round,
As soft as snow flake on the ground ;
And friends look on her sweet repose,
As on a summer evening's close.

The holy calm that settles round,
Is proof another world is found ;
And *this,* so full of care and strife,
No longer 's object of her life.

Oh ! what 's the busy world to one
On whose spring time the setting sun
Hath cast its shadow !—a wide stage
With mortals fill'd on pilgrimage !

The shifting scenes of life but seem
The dim remembrance of a dream :
How few those scenes on which we look,
Live in the page of memory's book !

Her spirit struggling to get free,
Pants for ethereal liberty ;
And all her hopes are fix'd above.
In realms of everlasting love.

No longer doubtful of her fate,
She lives for her immortal state :
With prayer and praise on bended knee,
She worships the great Deity !

She, like a distant sail at sea,
Glides from our watch-tow'r gradually
And as th' horizon shuts our view,
The meeting heavens enshrine her too.

The mystery of Death is o'er,
And doubt and dread perplex no more :
Her spirit hence has taken flight,—
But where's ! unknown and veiled from sight.

To scale Creation,—search the skies,—
Imagination vainly tries ;
To find Eternity and Fate ;
Intent to learn our future state.

Where highest solar systems roll,
And lowest depths we seek the soul!
And while the map of heaven we trace,
Eternity is found in Space!

Illimitable! vast! profound!
A vacuum without a bound!
Where planetary systems rise,
And worlds look mere specks in the skies!

No sign of change! no trace of Time!
But fix'd, perpetual, and sublime!
The work of an Almighty power,
Whom all with one consent adore!

Transported to some heav'nly sphere,
Souls cannot hold communion here,
The sacred Future to reveal;
For Death alone can break its seal?

TRANSFORMATION.

As mountain springs and silver streamlets glide
To tidal rivers and to oceans wide ;—
So human life in channels passes by
To the dark open of Eternity !

As when the evening shadows gather round,
And the soft twilight flickers on the ground ;—
Her soul withdrew its warm inspiring light,
And curtained up those glassy orbs of sight.

As when the distant strains of music rise,
And the deep echo of the hills replies ;
A supernatural voice foreboding fate,
Summons the soul to its ethereal state !

As when the last faint murmur of the breeze,
Is heard to linger in the quivering trees ;
The nervous spirit, ere it joins the blest,
Gives one convulsive throb and quits its nest.

As emigrant forsakes his father land,
Seeks a new country by description grand :
So Marianne calmly settling both in view,
Gives up the old world and flies to the new.

As 'neath the horizon day retires to sleep,
And sets the lamps of night their watch to keep ;
So we her setting sun and absence deem
A short eclipse,—an evanescent dream !

As when the seed embedded in the ground,
Swells and bursts through the husk that hems it round ;
The human germ, impatient for its birth,
Struggling for freedom 's born a child of Earth.

Exhausted nature sinks and pants for breath,
The bud of promise proves the mother's death !
Affection, joy, and hope, appeared in sight,
A few short hours, when all was hush'd in night.

Her nobler part, pure, vapoury and free,
Ascends to join in tuneful harmony
The swelling chorus of the Saints above,
To the all merciful,—the God of love !

What distant latitudes,—what depths profound !
What space those dim eternal regions bound !
What other worlds to pass ! what skies to clear !
Time must run out ere we can reach that sphere !

Inspired by their creations bards have been,
And vision'd forth the blest Elysian scene :
And artists, too, have pictured heaven, and drew
The angel state of being down to view !

What that state is and where, no one can tell !
The invisible hereafter holds its spell
O'er mind, imagination, reason, sight,
Bewildering all with vacancy and night !

Death is the barrier through which we must pass
To spiritual regions ; science has no glass
To search the undiscovered fields of space ;
Nor chart the lines to track the hidden place !

Yet like the faithful compass that ne'er veers,
The thoughtful mind to one point ever steers !
In wandering mazes lost, the soul may roam,
Still natural instinct guides it to its home !

OUR MISSING FRIEND.

AN ELEGY.

———

Her memory like a shadowy dream,
    Floats dimly through the mind ;
And like the wreck o'erflowing stream,
    Some fragments leaves behind.
O'er these we fondly musing dwell,
Since she has ta'en her last farewell !

Throughout the volume of her days,
    Her narrative we trace ;
And all we can admire and praise,
    While looking in her face ;
As when we knew it lit with smiles
Of gladness in these sunless isles,

How many scenes we linger o'er,
    With pleasure and delight,
And sigh to think we can't restore
    Our best beloved to sight !

To share those bright,—those earthly joys
The mowing hand of Death destroys.

Another tie of life is gone ;
  A tear o'erflows the eye :
Deserted, we seem left forlorn
  To bury those who die !
If we recall a few brief years,
A generation disappears !

How many hearts that once were gay,
  Buoy'd up with hope and song ;
Have like a vision pass'd away !
  Cut off from those among
They journey'd with in youthful spring,
And in their tombs are withering !

We walk in paths where they have trod,
  Repeat what they have said,
And with full hearts approach the sod,
  That marks their narrow bed :
And while engaged in silent prayer,
' A still small voice' is whispering there.

Our hope is in Eternity,
  To meet those friends again ;
When life is Immortality,
  Unfetter'd by the chain
Of brief existence here below,
No future change to undergo !

Affliction there will not intrude,
  Or grief consume the heart ;
Nor passions fierce to be subdued,
  Or conquering Death to part :
But soul with soul be link'd in love,
In unknown latitudes above !

Though fame or fortune spread renown,
  On life's capricious road ;
Our only record is a stone,
  That tells of our abode,
When we shall all have pass'd away,
Like beings of a former day !

As ocean tides rush to the shore,—
  As day succeeds to night,—

So Man, till Time shall be no more,
  From earth will take his flight ;
For like the wind impell'd he goes,
But where his destiny, who knows?

OUR LITTLE PET.

HER little round of life is past,
   Her angel spirit fled !
On her remains we've looked our last,
   And tears of memory shed.
So swarming Nations passed away,
   Now vision'd as a dream ;
So all things hasten to decay
   Down life's oblivious stream !

At opening dawn in youthful Spring,
   When flowers perfume the gale,
And passage birds return to sing,
   Where warmer skies prevail :
When trees put forth their maiden bloom
   Of promise for the year ;
A withering blight,—an early tomb,
   In sorrow found us here.

Her artless innocence and love,
　And sweet engaging ways,
Were emblems of the blest above,
　Foreshadowing her days.
The simple, chaste and pure e'er win
　Th' affections of our kind ;
For they reflect the soul within,
　And the angelic mind !

The crimson flush upon the cheek,—
　The quivering in the breast,—
The sensitive of mind bespeak,
　And modesty express'd.
Too delicate for sunbright eyes,—
　Too meek to dwell below ;
She left for more congenial skies,
　The inner world to know !

Ah ! life is such a fleeting thing,
　We scarce can call it ours ;
For youth and age alike take wing,
　In a few transient hours !
And while we weep at others' fate,
　And loss of friends deplore ;

We 're shortly mentioned as ' the late,'
   Lamented and sigh'd o'er !

Her image flits across the mind.
   As if she lingered near :
We look where we were wont to find,
   And half believe we hear
Her timid voice ! small things recall ;
   She haunts our dreams at night ;
Not like the shadow on the wall,
   But bodied forth to sight !

Who has not lost, ' to memory dear,'
   Some much beloved friend ?
Who has not shed a silent tear,
   And paused on his own end ?
When blotted from Creation here,
   His vital spirit flies
To undiscovered regions, where
   God's chosen never dies !

That much conjectured heav'nly state,
   We would give worlds to know !

M

'Tis wisely hid ! the book of fate
   A problem is below !
Prolific fancy loves to soar
   Beyond the milky way ;
Where Time's chronology 's no more,
   But one Eternal Day !

THE NIGHT LAMP.

Behind yon hills the sun has set,
　　And left its streaks of glory there ;
While in heav'n's arch in concert met,
　　The stars their nightly watch prepare.

The glimmering twilight steals away,
　　And gathering vapours dim the sight,
Extinguishing the beams of day,
　　O'ershadowed with the wings of night.

Without, the crescent Moon is slung,
　　To guide the traveller on his way ;—
Within, a glare of fire-light 's flung,
　　To chase the tedious hours away.

Enclosed within our curtain'd rooms,
　　Where in soft slumbers we repose,
The modest burning lamp illumes
　　Our darkness when we restless doze.

This faithful vigil of the night,
　Companion to the chamber'd sick,
Cheers with its little flickering light,
　As does the clock's alarm or tick.

In sweet communion with her God,
　The whispered prayer ascends on high.
Her future spiritual abode;
　For saint-like she prepares to die.

The weary sufferer sinks to sleep,
　Losing all consciousness of pain,
In still repose! oblivion deep!
　Which calms and lulls the aching brain.

Her dreamy fancy fills the air
　With seraphs in their flowing robes,
Whose harps and voices blended there,
　Are beckoning her to yonder globes.

'Tis like a guardian angel here,
　Watching the slumberer's passive hours;
Returning consciousness to cheer,
　And glad the sight with fragrant flowers.

Before the Sun at break of day,
   The tiny lamp grows dim and pale;
It faintly gleams and fades away,
   Like yonder distant Ocean sail.

How long and wearisome the hours
   Pass'd in the chambers of the sick !
A lull precedes the storm that lours,
   An omen in that death-watch tick !

How dismal is that dying groan !
   Her spirit flashes through her eyes !
Her pulse beats slow,—her breath is gone !
   And there insensible she lies !

THE SPECTRE.

In the grey shades of evening,—the dusk of twilight,
When the moon is on watch like a warder of night ;
When the atlas of Heaven with its stars is unfurl'd,
And the black pall of death is thrown over the world ;
When man has retired from the toil of the day,
And all but remembrance seems fading away ;
The earth looks deserted, its tenants all fled,
Asleep and unconscious as if they were dead !
Oh ! this is the all hallowed season to find,
Alone in their studies, the wakeful of mind ;—
The wrestler of thought, and the genius sublime,
Whose ideal creations anterior to Time,
Like the work of enchantment, when internal sight
Steals over our senses like a dream of the night ;
When the soul in a trance deserting us here,
Is viewing Creation from some higher sphere !
Abstracted, absorbed in reflection, the eye

Sees a flick'ring light passing suddenly by ;
Which slowly recedes as we onward advance.
But dodges our steps like a ghost of romance ;
And haunting our fancy entwines like a spell,
As if it had something mysterious to tell.
The phantom we view through the mist of the eye,
Looks on with emotion and heaves a deep sigh ;
As if it had known us and seen us before
It was summon'd hence to the shadowy shore !
Now it lingers,—now leads,—and ascending above,
Invites us to join ;—and we instinctively move.
All curious to learn, absorbed we pursue,
Intent at all risks this fixed world to break through,
For a glimpse of the next, however remote,
Which we can't conjure up in the flashes of thought ;
And whither our fancy continually flies,
As it glasses itself in the innermost skies ;
Which it peoples with shades of a multitude vast,
That have through the death gates of our planet past.

Shut out from the world, not a whisper or word,
In the deep solemn silence of midnight is heard,
Not a life breath is near to soothe or console,
The pensive ideas of a sensitive soul.

How solitude frowns as we look o'er the deep,
Alone on the shore, with all life wrapt in sleep !
Like those in their grave-clothes who withering lie,
Heap'd up in the fields of Death's cemetery ?
Who paid the great debt of nature and fled
To the regions of fancy and light overhead ;
Where the veil of the future, too sacred and bright
For vision of mortals, thrown over our sight.
Eternity's broad, boundless space is before,
A mirage in the desert,—a receding shore !
An ever hereafter,—yet now everywhere,
Like the viewless wind, or an echo of air !
From whence is this wandering spirit of light,
Revisiting earth in the darkness of night ?
Perchance 'tis the shade of some friend we held dear,
Impatient to guide us to some better sphere !
Where all that invention or fancy e'er drew
Of th' invisible world is unfolded to view !
It may be our Genius descended in love,
It may be a herald to summon above !
It flits,—disappears,—but again is in sight ;
Like a will-o'-the-wisp in a thick misty night,
Which glimmers and flies like an electric spark,
That vividly flashes past us in the dark ;

Mysterious it comes, and timid with fears,
Apprehensive, alarm'd, at once disappears
Down the gulf of oblivion! it seems to have past,
And, if apparition, has vanished at last!

A SIGH FOR THE DAYS THAT ARE GONE.

To look back on our youthful prime,
    When all was beaming bright ;
And mark th' invasions of old Time,
    Is morn compared to night !

'Tis pleasing to recall the past
    Of life and budding Spring ;
Though it be dim and overcast
    With Time's dark shadowing.

When all was innocence and love,—
    Our path strewed o'er with flowers ;—
When we were smiled on from above,
    And happy passed the hours.

When childhood's prattling tongue ran wild,
    On every new-born joy ;
And trifles light as air beguiled
    The restless, playful boy.

When hope was buoyant,—spirits gay,
　　Unclouded yet with care;
When smiles of gladness cheer'd our way,
　　And all was fresh and fair.

Our childhood 's like a running stream,
　　That swiftly passes by;
And memory of it but a dream
　　That fades but cannot die.

'Tis like a glorious summer day,
　　All lovely and serene;
When with our little friends we play
　　Upon the village green.

At evening soirée,—Christmas cheer,
　　The merry laugh went round:
The ball or show throughout the year,
　　Amusement for us found.

Oh! these are dreams worth ling'ring o'er,
　　And not to be forgot:
The magic wand should these restore,—
　　The cloudy parts should blot.

The poetry of life is here,—
  Its harmony and song ;
The heaven below of all that 's dear,
  To memory belong !

How interesting is our birth,
  How fairy-like we seem !
It is the music-time of mirth,
  The hopeful mother's dream !

The nestling is the parents care,
  Who watch it night and day ;
And for it every danger share,
  Ere fledged it flies away.

The buds of promise op'ning spread,
  And flower and fruit succeed :
The sheltering oak that rears its head,
  Was once an acorn seed !

If into times remote we leap,
  The world was but a speck !
And torpid as an infant's sleep,
  Ere it became a wreck !

Nations from individuals grew ;—
 Empires from hamlets rose ;—
Oceans from streams ;—the old from new,
 Each changes as it grows.

As passing o'er the bridge we view,
 An open prospect round ;
The charming landscape rises new,
 And life's a garden found.

When youth comes budding into thought,
 More staid and steady grown ;
School'd, disciplin'd, well train'd and taught,
 With manly air and tone :—

The fallow mind is planted now,
 And stock'd with new ideas ;
Studious and hungry to know,
 The world of former years !

How memory loves again to pore,
 O'er these dissolving views ;
As if it would the past restore,
 Which we so quickly lose.

We feel an interest in the young
   And new of every race :
And minstrels in all times have sung,
   Their heavenly dwelling place.

The part of life's enchanted ground,
   The home of ripening years,
Is in the varied landscape found,
   Like April's smiles and tears.

'Tis like an old friend's face we knew,
   Who left for foreign skies ;
Returning after years : we view,
   But scarcely recognise.

The golden hours of youth are fled,
   The harvest time of joy ;
And feelings that we felt are dead,
   Or mixed with base alloy.

All have their dark and sun-bright days,—
   Their stations on the road :
And from life's summit backward gaze
   On all the paths they trod.

Oh ! what a gap there lies between
    The dates of child and man !
How changed in feature, form, and mien,
    Since Life's voyage first began.

The beautiful remains of art,
    Relics of bygone time ;
Awake emotions in the heart,
    Like our departed prime.

How like a ruin ivy-hung,—
    A spectre of the past,—
Is venerable Age among
    The youthful living cast !

To see the withering touch of Time,—
    When blind and deaf with age,—
To look back on our early prime,
    When moving off Life's stage ;

Are signs of our approaching fate,
    Whom chance has left behind ;
Waiting like pilgrims at the gate
    Eternal ! old and blind.

At evening's close, if we review
   The shoals and quicksands past
Of being, our life looking through,
   Amazed we stand aghast !

All things at last, in turn, declare
   That Time is on the wing ;
Decay and ruin everywhere,
   Death's shadows round us fling !

THE PORTRAIT GALLERY.

How many things we daily see and hear,
And trust to memory will soon disappear,
And when departing scarcely leave behind
A shadow of remembrance in the mind !
Hence to preserve to future times and men
The voice of hist'ry, we unsheath the pen,
And aught that of antiquity remains
Recorded thus, our library contains :
Lo ! the dear relics round our gallery hung,
The lineage of those from whom we sprung ;
Saved from the general wreck and waste of years,
A regiment of our ancestors appears ;
Whose names and portraits, since they are no more,
We with a sacred reverence adore.
Allied by blood we fondly love to trace
The ancient line of our ancestral race,
And find a family likeness in each face.

N

Each looks upon us with admiring eyes,
And in their look our own we recognise.
Not all alike will our attention claim,
For we are partial as regards their fame.
The martial spirit, who to battle flew
Whene'er the trumpet of his country blew,
Looks proudly in his military 'tire,
Which damsels in their teens so much admire.
The privy councillor who served the state,
The doughty knight, and honour'd magistrate,
And that illustrious gentleman the squire,
Who ruled the village as a king empire ;
Are here assembled in their age's guise,
For their posterity to criticise.
That righteous prelate, in his silken gown,
Thought more of others' wants than of his own !
The good old pastor earned an honest fame,
And all who knew esteem'd and bless'd his name.
Yon beardless youth of melancholy mood,
Shunn'd the gay world and courted solitude ;
His arduous studies promised to illume,
But slow consumption brought him to the tomb.
And here amidst the unforgotten dead,
The female branches rear their flow'r-deck'd head ;

The maiden, blushing like an infant rose
Displays fresh beauties as she ripening grows,
She like a winsome woo thing standing by,
Smiles on her grave and bearded ancestry.
The cherub group in clusters round the chair,
Are faithful copies of their parents there !
Each cheerful face expressive of its bliss,
Looks sweetly up to supplicate a kiss ;
With tenderest love she hugs them to her breast,
And all the mother in her is confess'd :
To grace of person,—harmony of mind,
A meek and lively disposition 's join'd.

To know his origin and trace his sires,
The nobleman ambitiously aspires ;
Consults the archives of his native place,
Arms, hist'ry and traditions of his race ;
Wills, title-deeds and registers of trust,
Wormeaten, rent, and coated thick with dust,
Examined with an antiquary's zeal,
The Norman lineage of his blood reveal.
In his research the family confide,
And in their breasts all feel a swelling pride.
Oft will they boast of their ancestral squire,

And serfs and villains of their feudal sire :
And that enthusiastic age admire ;
When crusades in the east were once the rage,
And nations sent their armies to engage
The infidels who Europe's power defy ;
When zealots swore to conquer or to die !
With what deep feeling interest they dwell
Upon the cause, and those who fought and fell !
The days of chivalry, and popish thrall,—
Monastic sanctuaries, and armour'd hall,—
The pride of archery, the chase, the court,—
Old English hospitality and sport :—
The splendid tournament where courage strove
To win fair ladye to the arms of love :
Arm'd cap-à-pie the flower of Europe shone ;
For single combat threw the gauntlet down,
Where princes and the fairest of the land,
The conflicts witness'd from the royal stand.

These mural monuments in gilded frame,
Are frail memorials of an ancient name ;
The household gods of their descendants, who
But wait a little to be hung there too.
Our absent friends and all we hold most dear

In life or memory are assembled here.
On him who lately breath'd we feast our eyes,
And half imagine he to us replies ;
The artist immortality bestows
On those whose faithful likenesses he shows.
The withering hand of death is on us all,
And the tomb closes o'er us ;—ere we fall,
Some anxious thoughts will occupy the mind,
About the trifles we may leave behind :
The richest legacy is virtuous fame,
The rarest relic is oneself in frame.
Look where we will the march of Time appears,
And human sympathy melts into tears :
The Gothic ruins, once the blest retreat
Of godly saints, lie mould'ring at our feet ;
The monuments of sieges in their day,
In ruins laid are crumbling fast away ;
The few remains preserved entire from birth,
Look like grim spectres rising from the earth :
These venerable fragments scattered wide,
Were once our country's boast, and fathers' pride.

MUSIC.

———

LIKE dreams which o'er our slumbers steal,
   When midnight silently draws near,
The heavenly sound of music falls
   Melodiously upon the ear.

All other sounds have died away,
   And all around is calm and still
As twilight when the silver beams
   Are lingering 'thwart the western hill.

It speaks a language all its own,
   In symphonies of those above ;
It drowns our worldly cares, and thaws
   Our coldest feelings into love.

It lulls our senses which are fix'd,
   As if a spell upon them hung ;
And restless thoughts that cross'd the brain
   Lie mute and motionless as th' tongue.

What tenderness it doth instil !
  Impulsively our feelings rise !
What sweet remembrances it brings
  Of sirens fled to yonder skies.

It tames the savage, and subdues
  The passions of the human breast ;
It tunes the soul to ecstacy,
  And soothes the heart that is distress'd.

Pathetic airs fall soft as dew,
  But deeply as a last farewell ;
Awak'ning memory from its doze,
  And feelings which the bosom swell.

How joyous sound the village bells,
  As through the vale their voices rise :
'Tis like the minstrelsy of heaven,
  Descending through dissolving skies.

Hark ! hark ! it heralds Christmas tide.
  And breaks our death-resembling sleep ;
Charming us in the dead of night,
  Like angels who their vigils keep.

How billowy its rise and fall,
　　Its dulcet softness,—organ swell ;
It thrills the nerve-strings of the heart,
　　Or ravishes it in its cell.

Romantic visions it inspires,
　　And sentimental feelings raise ;
Till in a trance we seem to live
　　In fairy land and halcyon days.

Its harmony subdues the mind,
　　And stills emotions of the breast,—
Illuminates the face with smiles,
　　By gloomy pensiveness imprest.

It is the poetry of heaven,
　　Diffusing influence through the soul
Like magic, op'ning to our view
　　Ethereal worlds which round us roll.

How sweet it issues from the grove,
　　How cheering in our solitude,
When the lark's trill is in the sky ;
　　Or Philomela in the wood !

Its plaintive sigh is in the wind,
  Its solemn murmur on the shore,
Its minstrelsy in insect hum,
  And deep tones in the thunder's roar.

It stirs the martial breast to war,
  When marching to the battle plain,
Amidst the din of blood-stain'd arms,
  And cannons' roar, and heaps of slain.

It draws the tear-drops from the eye,
  Exhilarates the lively dance ;
It animates the noble chase,
  And th' excited steed to prance.

It peals along cathedral walls,
  Filling the empty space with sound
Of infant voices' sweetest strains,
  Or age's hoarse notes echoing round.

It fills us with devotion there,
  All meek and holy and sincere ;
Our sacred best of feelings flow,
  Mingling bright hope with timid fear.

The whole soul hangs upon the lips
   Of lovely woman when she sings!
Enraptur'd we scarce seem to breathe,
   When she her witchery round us flings.

The infant's cry is lull'd to sleep
   While cradled in its mother's arms,
By her melodious soothing voice,
   And her mesmeric magic charms.

APOSTROPHE TO A HUMAN SKULL.

Alas ! poor skull, who dared to disinter
Thee from thy sepulchre ? the final home
And destiny of man's terrestrial reign !
Thou apparition of the living man,
And representative of that we dread,
Couldst thou reveal all I would wish to hear,
Then thou wouldst tell the period of thy death,
And travel o'er thy pilgrimage again,
Narrating thy brief history while here !
This cannot be ! oblivion was thy doom,
Though thou didst strut with noise upon the stage
That we inherit from you ;—you from times
Remote and generations long extinct.
How changed from what thou wert !—thy dearest friends
Would fail to recognise thee in disguise !

Assembled in these gloomy catacombs,
Thy skull companions ranged in tiers around,
(Like a museum of grim and spectral heads)

Gaze like the listeners of a crowded hall ;
Anxious to hear the sound of human voice
Break on the solemn silence of the vault.

We look on thee as one who walked the earth,
And fed upon the vital air we breathe ;
Who felt the influence of the summer sun,
And all the seasons' changes as they roll.
We would inquire thy pedigree and place,
And how the world behaved itself to thee :—
If nursed in poverty's or plenty's lap ?
If bred in affluence, or obscure thy lot ?
And what thy fortune through the chequer'd scenes
Of life's eventful stage ?—how spent the hours
As each succeeding year fill'd up thy days ?
And what the circumstances of thy death ?
Oh ! could remembrance stamp upon thy brow,
And life's warm current glow upon thy cheek,
Those eyeless orbs flash fire,—that lock'd jaw break
The silence of the tomb,—inspire thy tongue ;
What interesting scenes and strange events
Would fill thy narrative while on life's road !

Ah ! shall we with phrenological skill,
Determine from the organs of thy skull,

The bent and constitution of thy mind?
Or with precision trace each organ's use,
And from this index fix upon thy will,
Purpose, or disposition ; we could tell
Thy weakness and in what thou didst excel.

All that thou wert we are ! and what thou art,
We must be ! this life is but a journey
Over a hill of loose disjointed rocks,
Whose ridge looks o'er a vast eternity
Of endless space, depth, and infinity !
Within our range, life's mirror here presents
The helpless infant crawling at the base,
Its safety watch'd with anxious speaking looks,
And tender feelings of a mother's love.

Another stage presents the jocund boy,
With colleagues mixed in recreative play,
Let loose from school the prototype of mirth.
All sunshine is ; no intervening cloud
Here casts its shadow on th' Elysian scene.

The next act ushers him upon the stage,
Just opening into life, when anxious thoughts

Begin to hang their signs upon his brow.
Emancipated from parental rule,
The restless ardour of ambitious youth
Impels him forward in his new launched bark,
And drifts him down the running stream of life
Without a compass. Where'er fate or chance
May cast his lot, he spreads his little sail,
And is into the sultry tropics driven,
Or arctic regions of eternal snows !

The fourth age comes, and finds the fire of youth,
With its ambition like a dim-lit lamp,
That has consumed the oil on which it fed.
Increase of years hath brought increase of cares ;
For now upon the bosom of the hill,
The man appears like Saturn in his ring,
Surrounded with his satellites of love ;
On him they fix their hopes and round him shine.
And in return he smooths their rugged path,
Shielding them from the world's malignant frown.
These with some other scenes of varied life,
Fill up the measure of his middle age.

The last and closing scene that ends the play,
(If he escapes the hidden snares of death,

Fatal to millions as they upward climb,)
Finds him a lone and solitary thing
Upon the rocky cliff! a chilling scene
Of winter wretchedness and human woe!
The siege of Time sad havoc there hath made,
And left the ruins on his snow-capp'd head.
Age, withering age, hath bow'd his manly frame,
His tottering steps supported with a staff,
And stript him of the health and strength of youth,
With every lineament deform'd and changed!
The twilight calm that settled on his brow,
And sweet serenity of evening's close,
Have shut their pleasing landscapes from his view,
For now th' horizon's light has sunk beneath,
And left him groping sightless in the world,
A prey to all the miseries of life.

Death's shadow soon around his couch is thrown,
And wasting sickness hurries on the foe
That sinks him in oblivion,—veils the past,
And opens on the future! depth profound!
A vast eternity! an endless round,
Of starry systems unrevealed to man!
The flickering spark of life at last dies out,

And he expires ! the grave receives the dead,
The curtain falls and closes up the scene !
And in a few brief years he comes to this,
The wreck and remnant of a living man !

THE CATHEDRAL.

Yon lofty towers, that top the country round,
Look like a beacon in the distance found,
And to the foreign or familiar eye
Are objects full of curiosity.
Their sculptur'd pinnacles and gothic dress,
With coloured lancet windows, all confess
The fabric to belong to Popish times,
When temples rose confessionals for crimes;
Their mould'ring walls and venerable cast,
Remains of Time, through centuries have past,
And with the dust of ruins round them thrown,
Leave an antiquity upon the town.

These proud creations of the hand of man,
Conceiv'd in fancy ere drawn into plan,
Attest the genius of a lofty mind,
Akin to that which heav'n and earth design'd;

And whose sublime conceptions form'd the whole
Divine machinery and th' immortal soul !

These gothic structures of the days of yore,
Recall the past, and Time's mile-posts restore.
On them we proudly look and fondly trace
The exalted genius of our ancient race.
With eager curiosity survey
The sacred relics of a bygone day ;
With interest listen to the tales they tell
Of feudal times and on their memories dwell ;
Their early chronicles and moss-grown wall,
A long forgotten age at once recall.

With reverence we approach their creaking doors,
And entering read their pav'd inscription floors ;
The storied window with its rich stain'd glass,
Who can in silent admiration pass ?
Adoring Saints around their Saviour kneel,
With looks expressing all they see and feel ;
The crucifixion serves to keep in mind
The idolized reformer of mankind :
The branching pillars, stretching through the aisle,
Run into arches of the pointed style ;

Up to the roof these lofty columns rise,
And there we fix our contemplative eyes ;
The sculptured screen divides the nave and choir.
And here we lingering look on and admire !
Our grand old race of monarchs side by side,
Renown'd for valour, dignity, and pride ;
Around the swelling organ tunes the soul,
And in its bass notes drowns and shakes the whole.
Reverberating thunder fills the space,
And drives th' affrighted soul into the face.
The service choir adorned with curious stalls
Of tabernacle work along the walls,
And closet seats beneath the gallery seen,
Are relics of what our old church has been,
The splendid carving of the bishop's throne,
The holy calmness round our feelings thrown,
The sacred altar,—oracles divine,
Preserved in stone, and treasured in a shrine ;
No offer'd sacrifice,—no incense burns,
But God's all-seeing eye its sunbeams turns,
With the loud anthems chanted to his praise,
The pious soul to its Creator raise !
The chapter-house preserv'd, attention draws.
Its tracery windows meeting our applause ;

The Library shelves are fill'd with books divine,
The hidden treasures of a lock'd up mine ;
The chilly Crypt with taper we descend,
And pause to think our miseries here will end !
The Cloisters next attract the stranger's eye,
And fleeting phantoms seem to pass him by ;
In human form they promenaded here
For healthy exercise from year to year.
Other memorials of our christian church
Are still preserv'd and open to our search ;
But chiefly these the curious engage,
With marble monuments of ev'ry age,
Which crowd the aisles ; o'er these we lingering pause,
Reading the stern decrees of Nature's laws :
The victories of Death, and man's brief hour,
How snatch'd from earthly honours, wealth, and power,
The virtuous, wise, and great, and all whom fame
Hath handed down with garlands round their name ;
The buds of promise, and the youthful bloom
Of summer withering in the silent tomb ;
The virgin flower and beauty ever dear,
Will thaw the frozen heart and draw the tear.

Should mem'ry awakening now descend
On some dear relative or bosom friend,

How will our sympathetic feelings rise,
O'erflow their banks and inundate our eyes!
O'er her we weep and picturing fondly trace
As in a glass each feature of her face,
Dwell on her excellence and virtues rare,
Her blest benevolence and graceful air,
Her cheering smile,—her happiness confest,
With all the gentle throbbings of the breast.
The only consolation 'midst our grief,
That softens sorrow,—ministers relief,
Is that we hope to meet our friends above
In realms of bliss and everlasting love.

ROKEBY.

We viewed the scenery around,
And felt we trod on classic ground ;
The craggy flood, and sylvan spot,
Alike are full of Walter Scott ;
His shadow seems to linger near
Each interesting object here ;
There's music in the fragrant breeze,
As it comes rushing through the trees.
These noble monarchs of the wood,
Invite to musing solitude ;
Amidst such charming scenes as these,
The nervous soul finds rest and ease ;
No worldly cares disturb its rest,
No passion agitates the breast ;
Serene, contemplative, and mild,
Nature adopts him for her child.
Here distant forests seem to meet,
Assembling kingdoms at our feet.

Here Lebanon's proud cedars rise,
And noble pines from kindred skies ;
The spreading chestnut's spiral bloom,
Sweetens the gale with its perfume :
With fostering care the ivy climbs
Up noble elms and fragrant limes :
The sheltering beech, with arms outspread,
Looks like a forest overhead :
In native dignity and dress,
All claim our praises with success.
The graceful shrub and evergreen,
Mix and adorn this sylvan scene ;
Here opening vistas glad the sight,
Through which the sunbeams shed their light.
Yon cluster down the sloping glade,
In contrast forms a friendly shade.
The group of oaks on yonder side,
Looks o'er a landscape rich and wide ;
A winding path through wood and dell,
Descending meets the Greta's swell :
Deep in the glen and hid from view,
The amber current courses through
Its rocky channel ;—far in shore,
Is heard its deep and solemn roar ;

It follows us along the height,
And breaks at last upon the sight :
No silver sound salutes the ear,
In gentle tone and accent clear ;
But roaring down, the rapid seems
Divided into frothy streams,
By beds of rocks which shallow lie.
Scattered in fragments deep and high :
O'er these the leaping cascades pour
Their deaf'ning thunder's shouting roar ;
The foaming torrent fierce and wild,
With rage o'erboils like Passion's child,
In whose tumultuous throbbing breast,
A fever burns and breaks its rest.
On either side its narrow bed
Rise verdant banks, with trees o'erspread,
Whose foliage adds a dismal gloom,
(As drooping cypress to the tomb.)
Luxuriantly wild they grow,
Diffusing solitude below :
Between their steep and rock-ribb'd sides,
The white-wreath'd river proudly rides.
Secluded in this lovely spot,
With life's dramatic scenes forgot,

The pilgrim strays, admiring more
The spot his fancy travelled o'er ;
Pictured in his creative mind,
And looks around in hope to find,
Some trace of genius left behind,
By Rokeby's bard ! a pleasing theme
On which the fancy loves to dream.

FOUNTAINS ABBEY.

ENCLOSED from public view the Abbey stands
In sweet seclusion 'midst romantic lands !
An interesting cosmoramic view,
Seen from the distant terrace window through !
Surprised we see this relic of an age,
Where pious brethren pass'd their pilgrimage.
Preserved from sacrilege, it now appears
In all the venerable weight of years ;
Fragments of stone lie scatter'd o'er the ground,
And ivy binds the crumbling walls around.
Where beauty's freshness shadows forth its prime,
Are soft decay and downy moss of time :
The gothic windows of exalted height,
Which shed within a dim religious light,
Are open to the cloud-encompass'd sky,
And to the hermit-owls sepulchral cry.
A mystic stillness o'er the ruin falls,
And fancy fills with shades its empty walls ;

The lofty tower which once to vespers rung,
And fill'd with grateful notes the whisp'ring tongue,
Is now an eyry for the birds of wing,
A lone, deserted, solitary thing!

Ancestral relics of departed days,
Will soft emotions in the bosom raise,
And move our sympathies as we behold
The spectral shadows of the days of old!
And like the monuments of Greece restore
A nation from oblivion now no more;
Between whom and our age a broader space
Bridged over Time, divides the human race.
A short eternity! a dreary night!
Ere half the world revealed itself to light!
Or infant Europe struggled into sight.

As o'er these ruins lingering we tread
Upon the sleeping ashes of the dead,
Time's hour-glass seems to measure out the span
Of life to nations as it does to man;
Raising them from obscurity to fame,—
From scatter'd tribes to an immortal name,—

From petty chieftainship to regal state,—
Illustrious, powerful, eminent, and great!
Renowned in war and flourishing in peace,
Heaven smiles and favours, and renews their lease.
Until the blood-stain'd sun gives signs from far,
And omens dire presage the coming war;
Weakened with luxury and declining years,
Some conquering hero in the field appears ;—
O'erruns the lands, depopulates, o'erthrows,
Plunders, destroys, exterminates his foes.
Their temples, altars, and their gods thrown down,
To smoking ruins he condemns the town;
Then leaves the wreck to ravenous wolves a prey,
And Time, which sweeps all earthly things away!

THE ECHO.

What voice is that repeating what is said?
Came it from yon lone charnel of the dead?
List to the sound! it mocks you word for word,—
" Who walks abroad?"—its solemn voice is heard!
Hear it again,—" the moon is in the sky!"
The very words are echoed in reply!
The deep and hollow sound sinks in the ear;
'Tis not the music of the voice we hear;
It seems to issue from yon sacred pile
Of ancient ruins, whose deserted aisle,
And roofless nave, once throng'd with holy men;
Whose wandering spirits stalk the earth again!
Ages have roll'd since this retreat they trod,
And knelt in worship 'fore the shrine of God!
But still their footsteps seem to linger near,
As by enchantment summon'd they appear.

Amazed we stand beneath the hollow rock,
And hear the deep reverberating shock

From hill to hill retreating like the sound
Of flying hoofs along the answering ground !
Awakening like the huntsman's echoing horn,
The pastoral meadow and the timorous fawn ;
And in the distance softly sinks and dies
In feeble whispers down the archway skies !

The air is breathless as the slumbering night,
Or catacombs of death, or meteor light ;
A mystic stillness hovers round the place,
Stealing us from the world to empty space,
Where restless spirits wander unconfin'd,
Viewless but self existent as the wind.
The supernatural voice and magic scene,
Are airy phantoms of what they have been ;
The ghostly spectres of departed days,
O'er which the shades of evening's twilight strays,
On which creative fancy loves to dwell,
Wrapt in the past which casts its magic spell.

'Tis like the dim remembrance of a dream,
Or floating clouds reflected in a stream,
Or voices issuing from the mountain side,
Or tuneful bugle o'er the waters wide ;

Or the repeating tunnel's rumbling sound,
Or labouring earthquake in the rocking ground ;
Or wild bird's scream as it pursues its flight
To woodland coverts in the drowsy night ;
Or the responses of a whisp'ring crowd,
Too full of feeling to be heard aloud ;
Or dying murmurs of the roaring wind,
Or melody that haunts the musing mind ;
Or the last groan from ocean's throbbing breast,
That swallowed up the shipwreck's crew distrest ;
Or the rack'd slave, or madman's dismal yell,
Or supernatural cries of ghosts from hell ;
Or sullen murmurs of the sea-beat shore,
Or bellowing thunder, and the cannon's roar.

REMINISCENCE.

To scan the beauties of our land,
   From King Lud city did we turn,
And following out the tour we plann'd,
   Hail'd the bright morn of our return.

The picturesque above the rest,
   With int'rest deep, the mind will fill,
And plant a wish in every breast
   To visit what is famous still.

But oh ! their fame will pass away,
   Like those renown'd in days of yore ;
And pilgrims visit in decay,
   Till Time shall know their place no more.

We see the withering hand of Time,
   Scatter'd abroad throughout the earth ;
And as we o'er its relics climb,
   Ransack their history, rise, and birth.

Monastic ruins ivy bound,
   And mould'ring walls of bygone days,
Will fix the stranger to the ground,
   And sentimental feelings raise.

The glassy lake's serene repose,
   The broad back'd mountain topt with snow :
The waterfall which wildly flows,
   And landscape scenery below ;

Will throw a witchery round the place,
   And stamp their image on the mind :
Which Time's screen will not soon efface,
   However far they 're left behind.

While these romantic spots we view,
   And picture glowing scenes to come,
Should fancy bid all these adieu,
   And light upon our distant home,

What pleasing hours shall we recall,
   What festive scenes shall travel o'er,
When maiden beauty graced the ball,
   And music wove its magic pow'r !

Or if to trace domestic bliss,
   In all its sweet endearing ties ;
The hour to think and feel is this,
   When man to other objects flies.

The carrier dove, by instinct's light,
   (Transported to a foreign shore,)
Circles the heavens, then wings its flight,
   And finds the nest she owned before.

So he whom other climes invite,
   Where scenes of interest long detain,
Will feel transported with delight
   To view his native land again.

A PRAYER.

Great Ruler of the Earth and Sea,
With rev'rence we draw near to thee :
And at thy sacred altar kneel,
To pour out all we think and feel,
In solemn, thoughtful, secret prayer,
Deeming thy Spirit's influence there.

Almighty Father ! we confess
Our earthly sins and helplessness.
Rebellious we have gone astray,
And so become the snarer's prey.
By nature we 've inherited
Infirmities ; and in us bred
Are dormant passions, which aroused,
Speak like the thunder in the cloud ;—
Which stimulate, enslave, impel
Our pliant nature to rebel ;

Fed by the vanities of life,
And all the elements of strife,
War, pleasure, pride, desire and gain,
And vices which corrupt and stain.

Creator ! Spirit ! source of all !
For help and strength on Thee we call ;
Sad, spirit-broken,—penitent,
And contrite-hearted, we repent,
And grieving for the past, implore
Thy grace that we may sin no more.
If 'tis thy pleasure or thy will,
With grief and trial us to fill,
To wean us from the world we love,
And draw us to thy realms above,
If this thy plan, ere set of sun,
In mercy let thy Will be done !

Teach us, great Judge, to know thy ways,
And from its mortal bondage raise
Th' immortal Soul to prayer and praise !
Inspire us with a life divine,
Let rays of glory round it shine,

Fill with intelligence and sight
Oracular, its wandering flight ;
And elevate with thoughts sublime,
Its destiny when done with Time !
With purer, nobler being fill,
And thy divine commands instil ;
Who reigns majestic over all,
Above, below, through great and small.

May we of life review the past,
And live each day as if the last ;
May conscience regulate and guide,
Through this world's rough and mazy tide ;
And every circling year contain
Some proof we have not lived in vain ;
That after we have pass'd away,
Like beings of a former day,
We may not be at once forgot,
As if we ne'er had been begot,
But leave our footprints here behind,
To bless and benefit mankind.

Great Being ! though to us unknown,
Thy Providence we freely own ;

And thank thee for existence,—birth,
And every blessing known on earth ;—
Our preservation, health and place,
And social comforts of our race ;—
For every mercy round us spread,—
For nature's gifts and daily bread ;—
For country, liberty and right,—
For earthly bliss and heavenly light.

In thee, great God, we put our trust
And confidence, for thou art just
And merciful, and full of love
Throughout Creation ! skies above,
Suns, stars and planets, Heaven's own choir,
Thy praises hymn, and own Thee sire
Of all the Universe ! while man
Reasoning from nature reads thy plan,—
As lord of the Creation, kneels
To Thee ! 'our Father' and appeals !
Hear, we beseech Thee, when we call
At morning rise or evening fall ;
Protect and shield, when buried deep
And senseless in the arms of sleep.

And when from that short trance we wake,
And life restoring sense partake,
May we for Death's great change prepare,
Though busied with this world of care ;
And lead a holier life below,
Walking thy paths where'er we go :
Let Conscience whisper, Virtue guide,
And Wisdom follow side by side.

Be thou our refuge in distress,
A Father to the fatherless ;
Implant in us thy righteous laws,
Ere sin committing may we pause.
Our first and noblest effort be,
To know ourselves and worship Thee !
Let self alone be not the shrine
We idolize as if divine ;
But may our faculties subdue
The ills of life in passing through :
Teach us to feel another's woe,
Inspire us to all good below,
And if the Lord has given us more,
May heart respond and help the poor,

And with th' afflicted shed a tear
Of sympathy while lingering here !
Oh ! let the curse of slavery cease,
And the whole world be bless'd with peace :
Make us contented with our lot,
And be our sins by Thee forgot :
Should Fortune's fickle smiles us raise,
To God (not man) be all the praise,
And if misfortunes on us light,
Reveal thyself, oh God ! to sight.

Save us from famine, plague and drought,
From sudden death, and foes without :
From epidemics, loss of sight,
And sleepless tortures of the night ;—
Mental disease, with fear and dread,
And all contagions round us spread :
Preserve us all on land and sea,
And teach us Lord, humility.
May superstition never blind
Or turn the balance of our mind ;
May we to others do as we
Would be done by, and honest be.

If we have enemies, forgive
And shew to them how they should live.
Humble our pride, and let us shun
Temptation, till our course is run ;
And then, when this soul's temple dies,
May it be wafted to the skies !

Soul of the Universe and Man,
Eternity with Thee began ;
Ubiquitous,—invisible,
A preternatural miracle !
Veil'd, infinite, and undefin'd,
The life of worlds, and light of mind ;
Whose spiritual essence is infused
Through Nature's life-pulse and diffused.
Reflected in thy works we see,
Thy greatness and sublimity ;
Imaged in distant Ages past,
Heard in the thunder and the blast ;
Felt in the conscience when we sigh,
' The still small voice' of Heaven is nigh.
The echo of thy voice is heard
Through the rent mountain-pass : thy Word

Inspired, extends from pole to pole,
And divine influence rules the whole.
Th' instinctive savage of the wood,
Invokes Thee from his solitude ;
And those who never heard of Thee,
Have sacrificed to Deity !
Enlighten'd nations own thy power,
Kneeling before Thee and adore !

EPITAPH.

BY sweet remembrance and affection led,
To hold communion with the withering dead :
Retired and private in a place like this,
Sacred to memory is spiritual bliss !
Where unobserved the mourner's silent grief,
In these sequestered spots may find relief
In pious meditation when alone,
And in recorded Fate may read his own !

DEATH.

His empire is the grave,
Which feasts upon the coward and the brave ;
    The monster who o'erthrows
Youth, beauty, sex and age, with friends and foes :
    We mourn, deplore, and wail
O'er our dear relatives, stone-cold, and pale.
    How long can we survive,
If fleeting time and fate thus onward drive ?
    Amid rude gulfs we steer,
Where treacherous rocks the flying vessel spear ;
    Tide, wind, may disappoint,
Yet, compass led, we sail to one main point :
    And hide our heads in dust
Where all our pride and splendour come to rust :
    Death 's oft a wished relief,
Annihilating misery, pain, and grief ;

Yet wears a cold stern face,
Frowning on ours and every foreign race :
Raging in the world unseen,
And passing away like a midnight dream.
Like the flickering life of man,
Without a compass, chart, or plan.
Mown down, the lords of earth,
With wealth, fame, power, or honoured noble birth ;
And triumphs o'er the slave,
With haughty rule o'erwhelming as the wave ;
Insults the freeborn mind
And tyrannizes o'er all human kind.

MELANCHOLY HOURS.

When hopes which have blossom'd are withered away,
   And the lamp of the mind is extinguished for ever,
Reflection succeeds like the twilight of day,
   And our thoughts in confusion are mingled together.

Oh ! then how the memory will feed on the past,
   And recall with a sigh all those moments of feeling,
Which vanished like visions of glory too fast,
   But imprison'd the heart in the snares round it stealing.

Oh ! then what a gloominess hangs o'er the mind,
   Which is laden with visions all misty and dreary,
As that of the madman, or prisoner confined
   In the earth's darken'd bowels half famished and weary.

The sufferer will pine who is grieved to the core,

    When all which affection has cherish'd is blighted,

When those we have loved we must never see more,

    By whom we 're rejected, forgotten, and slighted.

Yes! those who have once felt this nursling of sorrow,

    With the mental derangement and grief-moistened eye,

Whose spirits depress'd shall not rise with the morrow,

    Bereft of all comfort, should lie down and die.

EPITAPH ON LORD BYRON.

HERE rest the ashes of a bard whose fame
Spread through the world a lustre round his name :
The flowers of fancy nurtured in his mind,
Sprung from that nursery to delight mankind.
He, like the sun, rose slowly into view,
Immured in clouds, and glimmering through the dew :
But left the frigid regions here below,
For other worlds on Heaven's exalted brow.
Admiring nations listen'd to his lyre,
And rapturously felt the poet's fire
Sink deep into their breasts, and homage paid
To him who in his narrow cell is laid :
Whose lyre is hung upon the willow tree,
Mourning o'er him in plaintive melody ;
Whose lay is but an echo of the past,
Whose harp is silent, and whose shade is cast

Before us as a vision, where we see
Earth's pilgrims hast'ning to eternity.
Thus all the great who to distinction rise,
Are but as meteors passing through the skies.

TO A FAVOURITE PARROT.

Sweet Polly! pretty Polly dear!
Thy prattle still rings in my ear,
Though perch'd and shrin'd in that glass-case,
With others of the feathered race.

Vain and conceited little thing,
Shall I your minstrel be, and sing?
How you would coax, and kiss, and love,
With all the fondness of a dove.

How beautiful thy plumage green,
With blue, red, yellow, mixed between!
Then thy coquettish, winning way,
With always something sweet to say.

Pragmatic, whistling, singing dame,
Dull echo oft repeats thy name;
For thy weakest point and folly,
And song's burthen was "Poor Polly."

Who was loudest, chattering bird,
In company and would be heard ?
Who brought the wilderness to mind
When screaming through the hollow wind ?

Capricious, peevish, jealous pet,
Thy loving ways we can't forget :
Returning home made thee rejoice
With outspread wings and calling voice.

When perched outside thy prison cage,
In dialogue thou wouldst engage,
And humorous be, and join thy song
With mimic laughter loud and long.

Though friendly, yet if stranger dare
To touch thee, thou wouldst scold and swear ;
And like a little savage bite,
Then in their faces laugh outright.

To scratch thy poll thou didst invite
The privileg'd, who had a right ;
Perch on their finger, dance and play,
And sing to music lustily.

But all thy winsome ways to tell,
Would take too long, and so farewell!
Though life 's extinct, we look on thee,
Enshrined in glass and memory!

MELODY.

THOSE joyous chimes! those joyous chimes!
Recall the past of happier times,
When home and its companions dear
Look'd gay and sunbright through the year.

If we their number now review
Of all our dearest ones, how few
To us remain. Alas! the best
Are summon'd to their heavenly rest.

And so 'twill be with you and I,
When underneath the turf we lie ;
That merry peal will yet ring on,—
That sun return which o'er us shone.

The seasons roll as heretofore,
And will till Time shall be no more !
The sea and land will change their place,
And future times our footsteps trace.

How musical and sweet they sound
O'er all the lovely landscape round,
Their clear and singing voices rise
In answering echoes from the skies.

THE VALLEY.

Sweet valley ! thy charms kindle pleasing delight,
Which over us steals and enraptures the sight ;
The bald rocky mountains arise and inspire
Apollo's sweet minstrel to waken his lyre.

The serpentine river that babbles between,
Through the white foaming rocks and bright raiment
    of green,
Is an emblem of life in its changes below,
And the mazes and wrecks which it meets in its flow.

Thy patchwork of garden which hedges enclose,
The stillness that reigns, and the tranquil repose,
With the kine in the stream just now drinking their fill,
And the flocks' tinkling bell on the brow of the hill,

Is a picturesque scene artists love to behold,
Fresh and gay as the summer that never grows old ;
Though like the chameleon that changes its hue,
Are the seasons that roll with their charms ever new.

Here Ceres presides o'er her rich golden grain,
Until garner'd in barns from the winter and rain :
Thy soft graceful slopes in their liveries vie,
And the fruits and the roots of our cottage supply.

The rugged ravine in the midst of the wood,
With the roar of the torrent and wild solitude,
All speak of convulsions anterior to man,
With floods and volcanoes ere order began.

The meeting of waters, and the waterfall's leap,
Down the glen's frowning mountains and precipice deep,
Wind through the rent chasm which ages have worn,
And bared the foundations which Cyclops had torn.

All around the bright smiles of yon luminous sphere,
With the emerald pastures in grandeur appear,
The skylark from heaven its glad tidings brings,
And the joys of its heart in a wild transport sings.

The small scatter'd hamlet that shelters the poor,
And the husbandman's farm with his ricks and his store,
Mark the spot of contentment where harmony grew,
With the village church spire ever peeping in view.

In love with the landscape you view and admire,
And warm with the subject into glowing desire,
As a painter or bard in his fervor of mind,
Is impress'd with the beauties left far far behind.

In this rural retreat, and the absence of care,
With pastime amusements and scented fresh air,
Retired we may live in an Eden of pleasure,
With the friends of our heart and the Muse of our leisure.

THE BROOK.

Conceived in the mountain and launched into light,
It crawls through the channel and bursts into sight :
Then threading and warbling right onward it goes,
With its sad plaintive music as softly it flows.

Tell me, pretty Nymph of the wood and the dale,
Thy simple, engaging, and innocent tale !
Who wooed and who won thee ?—if happy thy lot ?
And whether thy union young streamlets begot ?

The mountainous rocks in disorder are spread,
Obstructing thy journey, and choking thy bed :
The full reservoir o'er the precipice sweeps,
And descends in a torrent in its falls and its leaps.

Assembled above us the waters o'erflow,
Then plunge headlong down to the chasm below ;
Through the clefts of the rocks into broken cascades,
Dividing but meeting again in the shades.

Enclosed in the passes, thy echoes' loud roar
Is heard when the floodgates their volumes down pour:
Excited with anger, all foaming and wild,
Until bursting with rage like a passionate child.

Oh ! say little wanderer, where art thou going,
Dreaming along without ebb in thy flowing,
And on what errand bound?—dost thou tribute pay
To ocean or river that crosses thy way ?

If swallowed up there and engulfed in the sea,
As a soul in the skies of Eternity ;
So chrysalis-like, now transform'd and new born,
On the wings of a seraph to God it has gone.

If thou, limpid stream, looking back could recall
The dawn of Creation before Adam's fall,
You'd tell how our planet first burst into birth,
With the earthquakes and floods and convulsions of
    earth.

How in embryo state there for Ages it lay,
Ere fully matured, when it sprang into play,
And on its own axis revolving it turn'd,
When the day and the night and the seasons return'd.

These cavernous earthquakes the Earth undermine,
When charged with foul gas in the depths of a mine ;
They swallow up mountains in vacuums below,
And entomb men alive and their cities o'erthrow.

In the caves of the earth, and the dark shaggy glen,
Pre-Adamite brutes left their bones in the den,
Long, long before Nature and Art had combin'd,
Or man had appear'd with his almighty mind.

Here Nature reposing, lies taking her rest
In a chaotic form,—in green vestments dress'd ;
But the Muses of Art with their sweet winning smile,
Shed a halo of glory round our happy isle !

The features of Nature and her sternness of face,
When embellish'd with Art, lend refinement and grace ;
So the cold of man's heart in his looks is express'd,
Until softened by love in the feminine breast.

A CHILD.

THE sweet little rosebud that hangs on the tree,
Is not half so lovely to look on as thee :
The emblems of innocence, beauty, and grace,
Are grouped altogether in thy pretty face.

Dependent and helpless this stranger of Earth,
His troubles begin soon as launched into birth :
Appease but his hunger, he sinks into rest,
And wakes to be dandled, and kiss'd, and caress'd.

The voyager gave signs of approaching the shore,
When quickened and wrestling for some time before,
New worlds to discover with freedom and light,
And a welcome reception from new friends in sight.

Modelled and fashioned is this miniature creature
In exquisite taste both in limb and in feature,
He clings to embraces which fondly entwine
As a tendril clings to the branch of a vine.

Oh ! list to the praises which o'er him are sung
By cherub admirers of eloquent tongue ;
An ' angel,'—a ' seraph,'—a ' darling,' a ' dear,'
Melodiously sound in the proud mother's ear.

Its natural instincts prompt to eat, drink, and sleep,
Like inferior creations, who bleat, whine, or weep.
He has not learn'd to think, remember, or talk,—
To read and to write,—or to play and to walk.

How helpless this pledge of affection and love,
Resembling a fairy from Eden above ;
A link in the chain that knits firmer the tie,—
The family pet, and their idolatry.

A glimmering light, like the rays of the sun,
Through the haze of the night at dawn has begun,
To light up with reason the lamp of his mind,
Where all was obscure, undeveloped, and blind.

As he ripens and grows, and increases in size,
So his mental ideas from their slumbers arise,
Like seeds of the earth as they burst into sight,
With intellect, thought, understanding, and light.

Thus equipp'd and appointed by friends he holds dear,
The journey of life is commenced in this sphere :
But who can foresee what misfortunes await
Midst the conflicts of life, and the arrows of Fate ?

STANZAS.

Who has not had friends and parted ?—
   Lovers who proved insincere ?—
Fickle-minded and false-hearted ?
   Such we 've known and once held dear.

Who has not his private sorrows,
   In this pilgrimage below,
Writ in hieroglyphic furrows,
   In the wave lines of his brow ?

Disappointment, grief, and trouble,
   And a crowd of ills beside,
Are but as an empty bubble,
   Floating on the ruffled tide.

From forefathers we inherit
   Lion courage and renown ;
And must arm with martial spirit ;—
   Or for ever be cast down.

We have duties that require us
 In life's battle to engage,—
Social duties which inspire us,
 To take part upon the stage.

Enter into competition.
 With the self-raised nobly great ;
Occupy their proud position,
 With rank, title, and estate.

Enterprise and emigration,
 From the old world to the new,
Have raised up a powerful nation,
 From the union of a few.

Be warm-hearted and ambitious
 To do all the good you can ;
Be both moral and religious,
 And a standard, model man !

Reverence wisdom, follow nature,
 And in Providence confide ;
Grasp the present,—leave the future,
 Taking reason for your guide !

When to Fate you have surrendered,
  Mourned by wife and children dear,
Thou shalt fondly be remember'd,
  And lamented with a tear.

THE END.

T. RICHARDS, PRINTER, 37, GREAT QUEEN STREET.

www.ingramcontent.com/pod-product-compliance
Lightning Source LLC
Chambersburg PA
CBHW030132060726
47499CB00015B/1641